TM

Guild Press of Indiana, Inc.

Indianapolis, Indiana

Field Surgeon at Gettysburg

A Memorial Account of

the Medical Unit of

The Thirty-Second Massachusetts Regiment

Reconstructed Fictionally
by

Clyde B. Kernek, M.D.

Original Illustrations by Clyde B. Kernek
and
Steve Armour of Alexander Graphics
Indianapolis

Guild Press of Indiana
6000 Sunset Lane
Indianapolis, IN 46208

Guild Press of Indiana, Inc.
6000 Sunset Lane
Indianapolis, IN 46208

Printed in the United States of America

Library of Congress
Catalogue Card Number
93-079618

Second, Revised Edition
May, 1994

ISBN 1-878208-32-2

CONTENTS

List of Illustrations

January 10, 1895

To the Committee to Erect a Gettysburg Battlefield Monument to Commemorate the Dressing Station of the Thirty-Second Massachusetts Infantry Regiment:

Comrades, three months ago you dedicated the beautiful monument to the Thirty-Second Massachusetts Infantry Regiment on the actual firing line on the stony hill near the wheatfield. I am both touched and impressed that you are now having a campaign to raise money for a suitable monument or plaque in honor of Surgeon Zabdiel Boylston Adams and the activities of his medical detail which ministered to the wounded men on the battlefield during that awful day of July 2nd in the late fratricidal conflict.

I have enclosed a map to show exactly where that dressing station was located. It is fortunate that Doctor Adams is still alive to enjoy this singular honor you plan. Few other surgeons in the entire War Between the States stayed so close to his men in actual battle as he did.

I take note of your intention to issue a memorial tribute book to Doctor Adams and the efforts of the medical personnel there on that second day of Gettysburg. I am honored to be asked to contribute my recollections of our activities there. Though I was but newly arrived, I had my own baptism of blood at that time, though the blood was not my own, but that of many brave men who fell defending the nation.

I have reviewed my own personal service diary and service records and have prepared an account of all my activities as a member of the medical staff in the Army of the Potomac. I trust you will pardon me if I include personal recollections and observations; I believed a full account would best suit your purposes and would also provide a memory of those trying but glorious days for my own family and posterity.

Your obedient servant,

Morgan E. Baldwin, M.D.
Formerly Assistant Surgeon
Thirty-Second Massachusetts Infantry
Second Brigade, First Division
Fifth Army Corps, Army of the Potomac

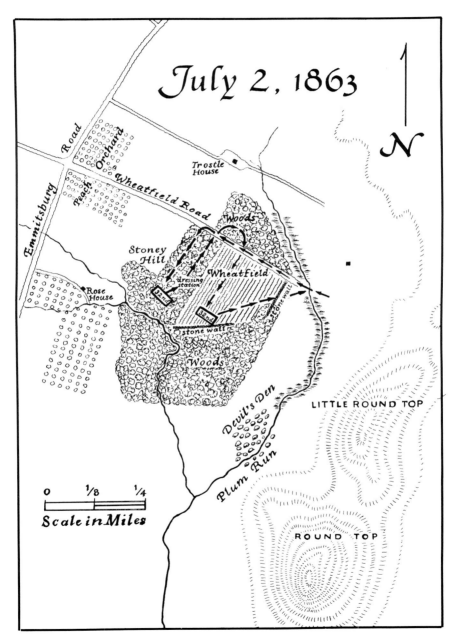

July 2, 1863

Emmitsburg Road

Peach Orchard

Wheatfield Road

Trostle House

N

Woods

Stoney Hill

Wheatfield

dressing station

Rose House

2nd

3rd

stone wall

stone wall

Woods

Devil's Den

Plum Run

LITTLE ROUND TOP

ROUND TOP

0   ⅛   ¼

Scale in Miles

Map by Richard Day

Chapter I.

Becoming an Army Surgeon

I was brought up in Hamilton County, Indiana, on a small farm just south of Noblesville. My parents had sacrificed to send me to seminary for a period of time; but I had quit because my calling did not seem to be strong, and the studies did not particularly interest me. It was Father's wish that I become a minister as he was, but instead I became interested in medicine while working part-time for an elderly physician, Doctor Samuel Hagen in Noblesville.

At first I took care of his horse and buggy and cleaned his office and stable. How well I remember that quaint old chamber, which was in the front of his fashionable home, with a special chair that reclined for pulling teeth and doing minor operations. Later he pulled me from the stable to assist in the office and to drive him all around Hamilton County for home calls. Finally, I asked him to teach me medicine and surgery, and this he was willing to do if I worked in his office full time. After about two years of this apprenticeship and reading all of his medical books, I felt the desire to try medical school. Doctor Hagen said he would help out with some of my expenses at medical school if I returned to be an assistant to him for one year.

My medical training consisted of two five-month terms of medical school in Cincinnati at the Medical College of Ohio, each costing $84. Even with the doctor's generous stipend the fee was still a significant financial burden on my poor family, because in addition to this cost, I needed their assistance to pay for room and board in Cincinnati.

Under dire necessity I left the Medical College of Ohio in March of 1860, and I returned home to Noblesville as promised for one year as an assistant to Doctor Hagen and to complete my training as a physician. Although this esteemed physician had not attended medical school, he had practiced medicine in town for as long as anyone could remember. He had seen about everything there was to see over the years and was considered the most experienced practitioner in the county for dosing, purging, and the old fashioned practice of bleeding. I hoped to gain practical knowledge and skill from him, and my only disappointment was that he did little surgery, and surgery interested me the most. He pulled many teeth, though, and that was always an interesting procedure. He was the busiest physician in Hamilton county and needed my aid, so I stayed on to practice with him after the year expired.

I resided with my folks at that time and helped Father when I could with the work on the farm. My primary desire, almost a burning one, was to learn surgery.

My practice was mostly medical, and the surgical part was primarily splinting fractures and doing minor operative procedures such as lancing carbuncles. Even most of the dental problems and pulling of teeth went to Doctor Hagen. I had a few medical books which I read when I had time in the evening by the light of the oil lamp. Good books on surgery were difficult to secure. Studying surgery by looking at drawings seemed useless, anyway, as I seldom had the opportunity to see or do these procedures firsthand. The most skilled surgeons lived in Indianapolis, and so most of the major operations were done there. From time to time I ventured into the city to observe these operations, but my hands itched to hold a scalpel to aid my suffering fellow beings.

In my continuing desire to learn the art of surgery, it came to me in 1862 that I could best learn as an army surgeon. The war started as I finished my year as assistant to "Doctor Sam," as his patients affectionately referred to him. Some good new books became available in 1861, and I bought *A Manual of Military Surgery* by Gross and *A Practical Treatise On Military Surgery* by Hamilton. These books stimulated my consideration of surgery; soon I conceived the notion that I could become a regimental surgeon in one of the Indiana Volunteer Infantry Regiments. Some of the doctors of reputation in central Indiana had become regimental surgeons and had gained honor and respect because of this service to the state and to country. As far as my personal commitment to the Northern cause, I believe I can say it was satisfactory for the situation. I lived in a county where Copperhead sentiment was strong, but I had always believed that the United States should stay united. Definitely I was no abolitionist, but then that was not a necessary concomitant of service.

I loved my country as much as the next man and was prepared to do my duty.

In September of 1862 I contacted Governor Morton to offer my services to Indiana as an assistant regimental surgeon. His letter to me regretted that he did not have a position for me, and I came then to the realization, since confirmed by experience, that such appointments were political. Regimental surgeons were the cousins and in-laws of the governor, and my family and friends were not political people; on the other hand Father was a minister-farmer, and, I suppose, a mediocre performer at both professions. We were poor and backwards by Indianapolis standards. I grew up in a log house, and the north wind blew through the chinks. Disillusioned, I lost the desire to become a regimental surgeon.

One cold, windy April day in 1863, the sheriff of Hamilton County paid me an unexpected visit. This fine gentleman was a member of the Blacksprings Baptist Church, my Father's church, and knew that I had been turned down by the governor for a position with an Indiana regiment. He said that he had been informed that the Army of the Potomac needed surgeons urgently, and he believed I should do my patriotic duty and serve my country as an army doctor, joining the army as a United States volunteer assistant surgeon. His kindness made my opportunity seem duty. Although the army needed surgeons desperately, I actually needed the army worse than it needed me if I were to get adequate surgical training.

So I signed the muster rolls of the Union Army through a Federal agent the last week of April in Indianapolis, 1863, as a U. S. volunteer assistant surgeon and became First Lieutenant Morgan Baldwin. The army would be sending me east to the Army of the Potomac, the recruiting agent informed me, where the need seemed more desperate than that of the Western armies.

Things happened quickly after that, as I had only a short while to say farewell to my mother, father, and sister Harriet, the neighbors, my patients, and my dearest Mary.

I had hoped by this time to have married my sweetheart of four years, but Mary was an independent young lady. She had been to the Ladies' Seminary in Cincinnati and knew Latin and music theory. She was waiting to see if I would be successful before she would agree to marriage, and I was attempting to reconcile myself to this opinion.

The day I left I stared at myself in the mirror wondering if the face I saw was one Mary could love forever. I was nearly twenty-eight years of age, clean shaven, with a receding hairline, unaccomplished, and essentially penniless. I was, if one were honest, a man of no prospects. My senior medical partner gave me only one piece of advice. "Don't use the blue pill. It may do more harm than good." That I had already observed at the college, but I was glad to have it reaffirmed.

The Federal recruiter met me in Indianapolis. He said he had a telegram from the Surgeon General. An assistant surgeon had fallen victim to the soldiers' disease, dysentery, and died rather suddenly. His regiment was in the Army of the Potomac and needed a replacement as soon as possible. Soon I was watching the cities of Southeastern Indiana speed by on the train to be that replacement!

I was filled with anticipation of a great adventure that comes not even once in a lifetime—the Conflict which had split our nation and the great battlefields of the Eastern theatre, about which we had heard so much. I should be seeing not only the elephant, but the giraffe! At the same time I felt a twinge of lonesomeness and wondered if I would ever see my home again. People were paying the sacrifice of blood out there, even doctors. Taking the B & O railroad across Ohio into Maryland, I eventually caught up with my assigned regiment in Virginia.

It was late in May of 1863 when I reported to Surgeon Z. Boylston Adams of the Thirty-Second Massachusetts Infantry Regiment. He was an experienced military surgeon, about thirty-three years of age, and would teach me well. I was eager to learn surgery and vowed to get the most out of this great opportunity.

Chapter II.

Marching North

May, 1863

The Thirty-Second Massachusetts Infantry Regiment, I soon discovered, was a fine unit of volunteers in Sweitzer's Brigade. It had been raised in the Boston area and had served its initial assignment at Fort Warren, where Southern traitors were confined in Boston Harbor. It consisted also of the Ninth Massachusetts, the Fourth Michigan, and the Sixty-Second Pennsylvania Regiments. Sweitzer's Brigade, along with Tilton's Brigade and Vincent's Brigade, made up Barnes' Division of Meade's Fifth Corps. Sweitzer's Brigade was at that time camped near the north bank of the Rappahannock River, along which both armies were encamped, nervously watching each other.

The battle of Chancellorsville, as is well known, had been a humiliating defeat for the Army of the Potomac in early May, and it was just at this unpropitious and somewhat discouraging time that I was coming into camp.

As the train slowed and cautiously pulled through a little village, Falmouth, gliding to a halt with a final lurch, I recall being impressed with the strong, well equipped army I was joining. All around me were seas of new tents and villages of supply sheds. I even spied a tethered balloon off in the distance. Bands at that very moment were playing and thousands of blue-clads drilled, marching and counter-marching.

The passengers of my train were mostly officers who quickly left the cars and soon were escorted away on waiting horses. As the train started to back out of the village, I realized that I was the only officer left in the area. Where was I supposed to go?

There was an ambulance wagon near the track. The driver called out, "Hey Doc, over here?" I lugged my gear to the ambulance and soon realized that I was going to have to load it onto the back of the ambulance myself. The driver remained there on his perch, his only activity being to spit a wad of tobacco juice on the ground. Thick brown saliva drooled down his chin onto his bushy beard. "You're the new sawbones, aye?" He motioned for me to hop up on the seat next to him. He said he was Private Jeremiah Hays and explained that he had been sent from the regiment to pick up urgently needed medical supplies and also me. He acknowledged that ferrying a new assistant surgeon was not authorized use for the ambulance.

The army ambulance was a wonder to me, and I found myself surveying it carefully during the ride. Special springs were designed to smooth out the ride over rough terrain for the wounded passengers. The front axle had one transverse elliptical spring, and the rear axle had one transverse and two longitudinal elliptical springs. The ambulance was light enough to be easily pulled by two horses; still, the ride was bumpy and uncomfortable even for the uninjured. I could only guess at its terrors for the agonized injured. It was, in fact, downright dangerous, and I flew clear off the seat many times and was required to hold on to the seat for the entire trip. Surely, I thought, the army might do a little better than this for our fighting men. The springs were too stiff. Perhaps it was designed more for durability than comfort.

It was Sunday afternoon, and a few church bells chimed the faithful to the last, or 1 p.m. service. The rough roads finally brought us to the camp of the Thirty-Second Massachusetts Regiment. Dreary indeed was the natural aspect of it when I arrived, I must confess. Spring was well established in Virginia; the land I had passed through was lush and green, but here in the cantonment of the Army of the Potomac there was not a blade of grass. The fields as far as the eye could see were dismal, all beaten down and thrashed by innumerable wheels, hooves, and shoes.

As we neared our destination, I saw more men and equipment, numerous batteries of artillery parked in fields, guns, limbers, caissons, horses, and men taking up a large area for each battery. We drove by endless tent camps of infantry regiments forming brigades which in turn formed divisions.

But the dismal Sabbath impression I received was not solely the result of so much cold steel and canvas. I knew I was in the midst of a beaten army—whipped most recently at Chancellorsville by Lee. I should pause briefly to note the attitude at the camp where I first landed. The senior officers I was to meet were unsure of the capability of the Army against General Lee's aggressive and well led Army of Northern Virginia. And I heard nothing but scorn and indignation heaped on the leaders, especially Hooker, whom they called "Pumpkin Head."

Faith in the mighty Army of the Potomac was dwindling, and many thought Lee to be invincible. It would appear to the world that the Confederate generals and soldiers were far superior to their Union counterparts. The civilians back home more or less thought so: the Copperheads had just had a massive rally on the statehouse lawn in my own state. I had witnessed it in Indianapolis; there had been fights between veterans and Knights of the Golden Circle. The newspapers were certainly not complimentary to the Army of the Potomac. I wondered what the soldiers of this great army thought.

Inquiring, I found the enlisted men and junior officers still had confidence in the capability of the Army itself and eagerly wanted the chance to prove themselves in battle. I reported to the commanding officer, Colonel Prescott, on that Sunday afternoon of my arrival at the encampment. He gave me a warm and hearty welcome and took me to meet the medical staff. In spite of my original impression, there was not a lot of activity to be seen as Colonel Prescott escorted me to the edge of camp where the medical tents were located. Two officers were lounging in chairs in front of a large tent.

As we approached they slowly rose to acknowledge their commanding officer. After some pleasantries, the colonel introduced me to Surgeon Zabdiel Boylston Adams and Assistant Surgeon Theodore St. James. Major Adams had a full beard as well as a full head of hair. His eyes were steady, and he initially appeared to be more stern than I later found him. Captain St. James was younger than I and wore his hair long. He sported a large mustache and had what I could candidly describe as evasive eyes. We shook hands, and Captain St. James took leave to check on a sick soldier in the hospital tent. Major Adams spent the next few minutes orienting me to my duties in the regiment.

"It is a little irregular to have a Hoosier surgeon in a Massachusetts regiment. Still I welcome your appointment," he said. Since the regiment was so desperate for surgeons right now, they would take just about anyone:

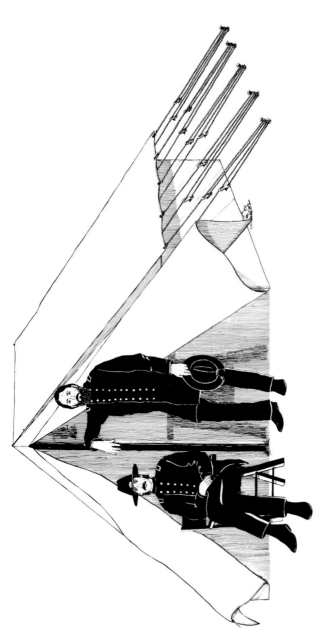

Two Surgeons Lounging in Front of Tent

either Massachusetts had supplied too many regiments for the Union, or the physicians in Boston were collecting so much in fees that they couldn't afford to be down here. Captain St. James was to be reassigned soon as surgeon of his own Massachusetts regiment. As I was a U. S. volunteer assistant surgeon, the plan was that I would later be reassigned to a general hospital or to a regular U. S. regiment. Surgeon Adams told me he thought the possibility existed that I could transfer to an Indiana regiment eventually. There was the Nineteenth Indiana of the Iron Brigade, the Twentieth Indiana in the Third Corps, and the Fourteenth in the Second Corps. And others were present also.

"I admit that I have volunteered for partially selfish reasons," I told him. To be honest, I said, I hadn't had much surgical training. I wanted to learn as much surgical technique as I could.

"Every young doctor wants to become a surgeon," he conceded with a smile. He asked me how much surgery I had experienced, and I confessed that I had done very little. During my apprenticeship I only pulled teeth and performed minor procedures to release pus. I had seen one or two amputations, and of course had observed a few other procedures in my regrettably brief stay at medical school.

"You will have to learn quickly here," he said. Then he reminded me that the army had just been soundly thrashed a few weeks back, and he predicted that Hooker would soon seek retribution. He thought that we might not have much opportunity for any surgical training until this occurred. "But be aware of this: when battle starts, you will be on your own. We'll put you to work just as soon as you get your possessions moved into Doctor St. James' tent." I was to report to this assistant surgeon so he could acquaint me with the cantonment.

I quickly picked up my gear, stowed it in the tent to which I was directed and went to look for my new tent-mate. I found Assistant Surgeon St. James in the hospital tent, a wall tent with the front and back flaps open for fresh air. There were six patients on cots; all appeared pale and lethargic. Assistant Surgeon St. James was standing beside a cot accompanied by the hospital steward and an attendant detailed for duty as a nurse. A sheet completely covered a particular patient, including his head. The other patients were too ill to notice what had just happened, or they knew but chose to ignore the death.

St. James had glanced at me. He was ordering the steward to remove the body, arrange for a burial detail, and notify the man's captain. After a short while, St. James, or "Teddy" as he was called, gave me a tour, showing me the hospital tent for the most severe cases. Four had dysentery; and one had inflammation of the lungs.

The deceased, it appeared, was an older man in his forties, a sergeant, who had been in perfect health except for occasional abdominal pains. The previous week he had developed moderate abdominal pain which was treated by blue pills to try to purge his intestines. Soon the pain became severe, and his abdomen became rigid and very tender all over. The poor man became unable to take any nourishment. He developed fever and a rapid, weakening pulse. All day yesterday he was delirious and talked to his wife, who was not, of course, present. Then today he died. His was a hopeless case; nothing could be done.

I wondered about a ruptured viscus, as I recalled hearing at medical school about a post-mortem investigation where a rupture of the gallbladder was found. Also, I remembered the words of Doctor Hagen back home—"Don't use the blue pill." Could this be a case of mis-applied medicine? Who was I, the rawest of raw recruits, to say?

We strolled down the company streets of the regiment and past the rows of tents. I could identify the group of tents as the home company of the soldier who had just died. The company's captain was explaining to his gathered comrades that a burial detail was being formed to inter the remains that evening. A private was handing the captain some of the dead man's personal belongings collected from his tent: some pictures, a Bible, a stack of letters tied together with string, and a pair of reading glasses. After we left that scene of melancholy, we proceeded past the other company encampments. These were quiet as the men were taking advantage of Sunday afternoon for refreshment of spirit after the dress parades.

Some, possibly the unchurched, played cards and were betting on number squares. A few of the men were writing letters home to loved ones. Tobacco was in wide use for chewing or pipe smoking, but few cigars, I noted. I was struck by the youthful visages of the enlisted men, although there were some older enlisted men with graying beards and weathered faces. At one end of camp the lieutenants, captains, and majors were sitting around in front of their tents taking the breezes and enjoying the benefits of Old Sol.

That day we visited the encampment of the Ninth Massachusetts, so I could acquaint myself with other of the surgeons in the brigade. On the way back I learned that Captain St. James had attended Harvard Medical School and had one year of training in Boston with a surgeon of repute. Well, he was certainly a very well educated man and confident beyond his twenty-five years, that I had to concede in spite of my personal indifference to the man. "Teddy" tended to flaunt his own successes and did most of the talking. I learned more about him than he did of me. In fact, he had not the slightest interest in my background, seeming to be too arrogant and ambitious to be interested in any other soul than himself.

In a haughty voice he asked me, "And so I'm to accept that you got by the Army Medical Board? Mr. Stanton must have forced the Board to lower the standards a great deal." I started to respond, but he interrupted, "I should tell you that the Massachusetts Medical Board complimented me on my performance. The highest score they had seen. How did you do?"

"I passed. I prepared scrupulously, and I passed," was all I could say.

He snorted disdainfully and went on. Now that I was here, he said, his duties would be shifted to the division level. He expected soon to be appointed Surgeon of his own regiment, his father being a good friend of Governor Andrew. The governor had promised him a regiment the coming summer. He had recently been appointed as one of the division operating surgeons during times of battle. "I will be with the operating staff of the division field hospital when the army is engaged," he said, with what I thought was a lack of gentlemanly modesty.

And as to my own duties, they would be routine in the cantonment, but when battle came, I would be joining the staff of the dressing station that Surgeon Adams would establish near the battle line. Once the dressing station was in operation, Adams would report to the division field hospital to help treat the wounded there. My job would be to stay at the front as long as needed to dress the wounds and send the wounded on to the field hospital for surgery.

"Usually dressing stations are set up just outside musketry range," he said. "A sharpshooter can hit a man at five-hundred yards, but the average soldier is accurate only at two-hundred. The bad news is that Adams likes to set up his station as close to his men as possible, believing it is good for morale and steadies the men. The last time our regiment was engaged, Adams and I were just one-hundred-and-fifty yards behind our line. That is closer than I prefer, but he thinks the men feel better knowing that their surgeons are there with them. You will certainly be able to hear the minié balls humming through the air. My advice to you . . . is . . . stay low."

I thanked him for the advice and asked who would be helping me while I was dodging minié balls and giving aid to the wounded.

"You will have an orderly with the medical knapsack and a steward to help you, and some of the drummer boys and other enlisted men detailed as attendants," he replied. "Stretcher-bearers will carry in the seriously wounded. The walking wounded will come in on their own." He was tiring of instructing me. "Remember to put out the red hospital flags for them to follow. After you dress the wounds and control the bleeding, you will supervise the loading of the ambulances that will take the wounded to the division field hospital for surgery. You will have at least two ambulances with you, and we can send you a third if needed." He gave me assurance that Division headquarters would send me everything I needed.

I remarked that that would be certainly reassuring, should I survive in the midst of the firing.

"You must stay with the regiment until they retire from the battle line. When the boys run out of ammunition, they will be relieved by a reserve regiment. Then you can retire safely behind the lines with them. Wherever the regiment goes, you must accompany them," he told me.

I inquired what would happen if the men were pushed back behind the dressing station while I was still treating the wounded?

He looked down his nose at me. "How fast can you run? Besides, a surgeon's obligation is to remain with the wounded."

As if I didn't know that. "But don't I get to do any surgery? I didn't realize I'd be under fire. They didn't tell me that I would have to run for my life."

He turned to me and said, archly, "Doctor—or shall I call you

Baldy? Baldwin, Bald One, good jest. I started out just like you. You'll get to do some surgery. When the regiment retires for the night, come over to the division hospital. First, they will assign you to dress wounds. All of us serve as dressing surgeons to begin with. Possibly they may require you to keep the medical records. Later, they'll let you assist with some of the surgery. You may get to hold the leg or tourniquet, or retract the soft tissues, or even give the chloroform. If you show them you have the basic skills to become an operating surgeon like me, they will probably let you try to do some surgery," So he told me, and peremptorily left.

I heard the sounds of a drum and finally identified the dead march. The burial detail was over at the hospital tent. The coffin for the dead sergeant was arriving from Division.

As I walked behind the hospital tent, I saw two orderlies drop the soldier's body into the wooden box. The top was secured, and the coffin lifted onto the back of a wagon hitched to two mules. Chaplain O'Mara, who served the brigade, told me that the deceased had no immediate family. Further, the dead man's most recent letter was bad news from his wife back home; she had deserted him. It was all too sad. The burial detail and wagon slowly moved out of camp to the mournful beat of a muffled drum. Our chaplain and some of the dead soldier's comrades followed, and the procession soon passed out of sight. Then, it was business as usual in the camp again. The Army of the Potomac could not pause long to mourn the death by disease of one soldier.

That evening I was invited to join the other officers of the regiment for supper near the commander's tent. Surgeon Adams, called Zab by some of the older officers, found opportunity to discuss certain recent military tactics. He spoke of flanking maneuvers, reconnaissance in force, use of artillery, and other tactics new to me. I watched him and concluded he could have been a naturally talented line officer.

The captains and lieutenants contributed their comments on their brief encounters with Rebels. To hear them, the Rebel soldiers were a dirty, uneducated, illiterate, wiry refuse pile of humanity, who also chanced to be among the best soldiers in the world. They looked neglected, but they behaved as well disciplined soldiers. The Rebels they described were fierce fighters who would hit fast and hard with a yell so inhuman that it was often difficult for the Union line officers to keep their men from breaking ranks and running for the rear. I could not imagine a sound so frightful that brave men equipped with the best Springfields and Enfields might think about running. The file-closers must have their hands full during battle with so formidable an enemy as these Confederate traitors. With interest I anticipated the day when I might hear this Rebel yodel, from a safe distance of course.

During the meal one of the young officers introduced himself to me. Lieutenant Barrows was from Charleston; he had attended Exeter Academy and had a most ingratiating and outgoing personality. He confessed that he was a Quaker, one of the few who had the persuasion that God wished him to fight for the freeing of the slaves rather than plead pacifism. I found him to be a very religious man who never cursed nor drank spirits. Later I learned that he was very well respected, considered reliable and steady under fire by both officers and men in the entire regiment. It was comforting to know that there were people like him in our military force.

Returning to the regimental hospital I joined Doctors Adams and St. James in watching the sun go down from in front of our tent. Surgeon Adams had Steward Franz bring out some whiskey from the hospital medical supplies for us to sip from tin cups. My welcome was official.

The steward, Ludwig Franz, was originally from Bavaria, and he was fully acquainted with the principles of pharmacy. He seemed very proud of his uniform, which he kept brushed and neat. His sack-coat had the half chevron of emerald-green cloth with a caduceus on each sleeve, and he always wore his forage cap when outside. He spoke with a thick German accent, yet I could understand his words, though imperfectly. Surgeon Adams considered Ludwig to be the best steward in the entire division and had officially commended him.

As we started to sip our whiskey, Adams speculated as to General Hooker's next move against Lee. He had heard that we might move out at a moment's notice. St. James, the steward, and I listened to learn what Surgeon Adams might know about our future orders.

He stated that General Hooker was "scared to death of Lee." But then he looked up at the northern sky as if pondering a situation beyond the war. "I am always more afraid of disease than I am of the Secesh. Two men die of disease for every one killed by Rebel bullets," he said. "The Medical Department could win this war single-handedly, if only we could control diarrhea. The Confederates would run out of men before we would." He looked me in the eye, noting my interest.

"It is a simple matter of mathematics. Sanitation could probably win this war alone, if given half a chance." I was curious about his practice in Massachusetts. He must, I knew, have had many years of experiences superior to mine. He told me he had been educated at Harvard and had taken up practice in Boston without experiencing much success for quite a while, but that gradually he felt his reputation had grown. He valued a varied practice, he said, and quoted many odd cases to me, ranging from hysterical women laboring under the beliefs they had odd tumors to men who had maimed themselves from guilt over misuse of their manhood. He had an odd turn of mind, valuing the curiosities of the medical practice, but that did not stop him from having one of the most deservedly fine reputations in the Northern Army.

We sat in silence a few minutes, each lost in his own thoughts. I had to add some water to my cup in order to choke down the warm army whiskey, which burned my esophagus with each swallow. Adams, St. James, and Franz took their whiskey straight. At length I discreetly tossed mine on a clump of trampled crabgrass. Whiskey was hard to find for most soldiers when the army was in the field, so this was considered a treat by the other three, but not by me at that time.

The sounds of the drummer boys at 5 a.m. signalled reveille. I watched from the hospital area as the men assembled in line for roll call and began boiling their coffee and fixing breakfast in small groups about the camp. The smell of coffee was good relief from the ammoniacal reek of the latrine trenches downwind.

On this, my first day on duty, Assistant Surgeon St. James and I accompanied Surgeon Adams and Steward Franz on rounds in the hospital tent. Some of the patients were improving and able to take nourishment. They were being fed plain lemonade and chicken broth. After rounds we assembled in front of the hospital area for sick call. Doctors Adams, St. James, and I seated ourselves in chairs under an oak tree with chairs for patients facing us.

Then I experienced my first sick call. A first sergeant marched a rather long line of men and boys to our front and had them stand in a straight line. It looked like an entire company was sick. I watched as Doctors Adams and St. James together examined each patient in order. Most complaints were for diarrhea, but a few had sore feet and wanted to get out of some detail. I soon saw that the soldiers had to be significantly sick before they could be relieved of their daily soldiering responsibilities. Some blue pills, big as hazelnuts, were passed out, and remembering again the advice of Doctor Hagen back home in Noblesville, I quietly inquired if they might cause more harm than good. Doctors Adams and St. James both glared at me, and St. James told me to keep my own opinions to myself from now on. But I felt vindicated when I later learned that the men usually threw these blue pills away.

The line was quickly worked down to the last man, and sick call was over. I lingered a few minutes to talk to the last patient, as he said, "Hello, Doctor," in a friendly manner and was a talkative sort. I learned that he was Corporal Jacob Phillips from the Berkshire Hills of western Massachusetts, who had joined the Thirty-Second out of his home county. He told me that after the war was over his dream was to attend medical school. I started to give the young man some encouragement, but St. James interrupted, "Corporal, get back to your post immediately!" There was, I saw, little opportunity for chatter, idle or not.

Next, St. James and I visited those patients bedridden in their tents, a large number as it turned out. One soldier had an intermittent fever and chills. St. James cursed that the whole division did not have one single thermometer. He put his ear to the man's chest. "Probably not inflammation of the lungs," he muttered. St. James thought the patient had ague (malarial fever) so the patient was sent to the hospital tent with a message for Steward Franz to put him to bed and give him a dose of quinine. "How do you know it's ague?" I asked. St. James never answered my question, but when I later asked Doctor Adams about ague, he told me it was not common this time of year.

St. James and I finished the camp rounds and walked over to the latrines. "—stinking sinks," he cursed. St. James explained that dirt was supposed to be thrown in the trenches daily. He exclaimed that it was no wonder the camp was rank and pestilential; he was getting sick and tired of trying to teach these "farm boys" sanitation. He instructed me to meet him back at the hospital, for he needed to reprimand the colonel about his filthy, smelly camp. It had been over a year since the Army of the Potomac had sent orders to regimental commanders to set up sanitary codes. St. James thought Adams was probably right that we could win this "d—d war" if we could just convince the "d—d brass" that sanitation was one of the keys to a mighty army.

Ten minutes later St. James returned. The issue of sanitation had fled his mind. He had been instructed that we had orders to move out early tomorrow morning. My orders were to get the supply wagon loaded in the afternoon. He offered to show me the new surgical instruments as we packed. "The Army has supplied our corps with the best amputation sets that money can buy," he told me. I looked on with curiosity as he unfolded the set.

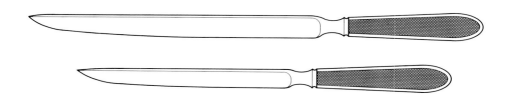

Amputating Knives

I was amazed at the array of instruments. The amputation set was the largest and best I had ever seen, a brand new major amputation set by Tiemann surgical instruments of New York City. The wooden case was well crafted, with compartments inside lined with plush red velvet. The instruments were shining, burnished steel, indeed the best surgical instruments that money could buy. Obviously President Lincoln was not sparing any expense for the Medical Department. I thought of what I heard of the Rebels' medical situation. These days, they said, surgical instruments were at a premium and had to be smuggled into the South. Perhaps the war would be won, in the hospital at least, with instruments like these.

Doctor St. James went over each instrument in the amputation set. The Liston amputating knives were long and pointed and very sharp along their single edge, and the Catling (Catlin) amputating knives had sharp double edges, so they could cut in either direction, with a sharp point allowing ease in pushing the knife through a limb prior to cutting the tissue flap from inside-out. There were various scalpels and curved knives. These new instruments were much sharper than the rusty, worn-out knives I had seen at home, and I yearned to use them in the beneficial exercise of my calling.

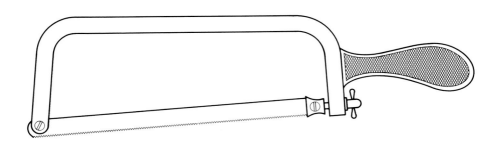

Capital Bone Saw

The bone saws consisted of the large capital saw, smaller interosseous and metacarpal saws, and a Hey's saw for the skull. I picked up a bullet forceps for extracting missile fragments, and handled a variety of dressing forceps, arterial forceps, scissors, clamps, probes, directors, elevators, tenaculums, and retractors. A Petit's spiral tourniquet was included in the set. Of particular high quality was the silk thread kept in the set for tying bleeding vessels and approximating amputation wounds using the large curved needles.

That afternoon we packed up the medical and surgical equipment and got the medical supply wagon loaded. One ambulance load of seriously ill patients was sent out that afternoon to start these men on their way to a general hospital in Washington via railroad. The regiment had to travel light and encumbrances had to be left behind. By dusk the regiment was ready to move, whenever the orders came down.

Only a day ago I had arrived, a greenhorn off the train. Now I was to be marching with the Army of the Potomac. I sat down to write letters home to the folks and Mary while I had the chance. If we were soon to be on the move, I worried how letters from home would reach me. Father probably was working too hard on the farm because I was not there to help him with the heavy work. Mother and Harriet would be out in the fields doing the work I used to do to help Father, and that was a matter of concern.

And cautious Mary, I worried how long she might wait for my return. Our relationship had become somewhat one-sided, and a young lawyer who had moved to Noblesville the year prior to this seemed to me to have had his eyes on her from the start. I suppose he was glad to see me leave town and was now squiring her about to the strawberry socials and the like at his church. How quickly we are forgotten, important as we seem to ourselves, when we are once out of sight. "Mentisental" thoughts commanded my attention for a time.

We did not move out the next day, as anticipated. Several days passed as we waited, ready to go. This gave me some time to study the few manuals and treatises that were provided on military medicine and surgery. I started reading Tripler and Blackman's *Hand-Book for the Military Surgeon,* but my attention was thoroughly engaged when I discovered Smith's *Hand-Book of Surgical Operations.* This textbook was just what I had been searching for, because it told in detail how to do the operative procedures I so yearned to undertake.

Smith's book started out with the basic surgical information which I needed to learn, such as the position to hold the scalpel while cutting tissue. The illustrations were numerous and clear, and there were three illustrations to show the positions of holding the scalpel. This surgical instrument, so it told me, is usually held as a pen for fine dissections and limited incisions. It can also be held with the handle resting in the palm and grasped by the thumb and the index and long fingers, lightly supported by the ring and small fingers, for making long incisions. The scalpel can also be held much as the bow of a violin for delicate dissections. What music would be played in that way! I looked carefully at the illustrations, fixing them in memory for future reference.

Dressings and bandages were also thoroughly described. The control of hemorrhage by tourniquet and ligature was well covered, including illustrations to show the surgeon's knot and the sailor's knot. Even anesthetics were discussed in this great text.

I was particularly enthusiastic about learning all of the various operative techniques for amputation of the various parts of the upper and lower extremities. For example, there were various techniques for amputation of the finger through any of the phalangeal bones or disarticulation through any of the joints of the finger. The fingers could be amputated by either the circular method or the flap method just as for amputation of the extremities at the other levels. Ah, I had heard of these of course, and received some basic introduction in medical school, but here were details for surgery right on the field of battle. The fine illustrations of the numerous operations for the amputations were clear and very helpful to me in learning about surgery. Surgical instruments were also well illustrated in the text, which I studied at every spare moment and decided to keep at hand for future reference.

Days dragged on in camp until the end of May. We had long since given up being on the ready. I continued seeing sick call, working within the hospital tents. My spare moments were occupied studying surgical techniques from books until that day when I could actually put this knowledge to practical use doing operative procedures on wounded soldiers. The daily drills were wearing, tiresome in the hot sun, and morale was sinking with each passing day. Then there was a rumor that other corps of the army were already on the move. The men were excited; perhaps something was starting to happen. During the evening of May 28, orders came down to prepare to move out in the morning. At last the Fifth Corps would be marching—in reality!

The drums rolled at 5 a.m. on May 29, with orders following to break camp. By early afternoon the regiment was standing in column on the road. Surgeon Adams was mounted on his black horse at the back of the column, with Assistant Surgeon St. James at his side, also on horseback. I had been instructed to ride the ambulance with our few soldiers too ill to march that day at the end of the division, the tail of the dog, so to speak. The medical supply wagons were with the other regimental supply wagons following the ambulance train like the tip of the tail of the dog. We were soon on our way headed west as a hot sun blazed down.

The spectacle was impressive but soon debilitating. The road was narrow and dusty, and thousands of pairs of feet kicked up a choking dust cloud. I could only see ahead to the regiment in front of the ambulance train, and the end of our train was hidden from view. Cast forth on this island of dust it was hard to imagine that we were a small part of a corps of three divisions all on the move at the same time in the same direction, as all I could see was the back of the last brigade and the ambulance wagons as the column moved down the dusty road.

The organization needed for the Fifth Corps to get these thousands of men and hundreds of wagons, ambulances, and horses plus five batteries of artillery moving was something to ponder. How did General Hooker decide where each of his seven corps was to go and which road to take? How many aids and staff officers were required to coordinate the movements of the nearly 100,000 men of the Army of the Potomac?

Now and again the stunned civilians of Virginia were visible along the way staring with wide eyes, holding up babies to look at the long columns of infantry soldiers, guns, horses, ambulances, and wagons passing by for hours seemingly without end. They must have wondered where we were going, and so did we.

CHAPTER III.

Reports of Battle

May 29, 1863

What direction were we going? My perspective robbed me of the ability to clearly discern direction. The road was a winding one, and the trees along the road often screened the countryside from view. One hour we would be marching west, then the next hour it would be east. We were marching north much more of the time than south. Of that, one could be certain.

The ambulance lurched and rocked on the rough road, and my buttocks were becoming increasingly sore. I couldn't understand why the driver never complained about his posterior. Possibly it was calloused. He just cursed when the ambulance train came to one of its frequent stops. The two horses pulling us behaved beautifully, and perhaps the driver was more skilled than I gave him credit for. Perhaps he made his job look easier than it really was. This was a rough ride for the two sick privates lying down in back, and I was sure that as soon as they improved a little, they would be glad for the opportunity to march once again with their comrades.

On rounding a bend in the road we came to another stop. The driver cursed as usual at the delay. I stood up to look ahead and saw that there was a Parrott rifle tilted down on its side blocking the road. The marching infantry soldiers had easily passed around the obstruction, but the passage of the wagons was impeded. Surmising that this was to be a long delay, I descended from the ambulance and walked ahead to the wrecked gun.

The gun carriage was down on the left side, the spokes of the wheel having broken in a deep hole in the road. Lieutenant Hazlett, commanding, I believe it was, the Fifth United States Battery D, was directing repairs on the gun. A spare wheel was brought from the back of a caisson to replace the broken one. I enjoyed chatting with this fine officer as he competently oversaw the righting of his heavy Parrott gun. Timbers were placed under the left side of the carriage so the spare wheel could be secured in place. A gaggle of artillerymen held the heavy gun upright while the timbers were slid in place under the left side of the axle. Once repaired, the gun was connected to its six-horse limber and was once more on the move. I returned to my ambulance and soon the wagon trains were again rolling down the hot, dusty road to who knew where.

There was a rumor that Lee was taking his forces north, but his specific intentions were unknown. We became thoroughly conversant with the Virginia countryside. The men began to grumble, and sick call became busier with blisters, sore feet, and sunstroke. Passing places like Barnett's Ford and Kemper's Ford, we began to wonder if Lee's Army had been absorbed into the villages of Virginia. It was certainly nowhere to be seen.

News came of a big cavalry battle at Brandy Station on June 9, where the Union cavalry made a good showing against Jeb Stuart's forces. It appeared that General Joe Hooker was finally going to confront General Lee. The Fifth Corps continued on the march in a northwesterly direction gradually easing ever northward, and I rested my sore *derriere* by marching part of the time at the rear of the regiment. This gave me a healthy respect for the men, each of whom had to march day after day carrying musket, knapsack, canteen, haversack, cartridge box, and bayonet.

Then, on June 17, the Corps made a forced march north for twenty miles under a blistering summer sun. Water was as scarce as ducks' teeth. Adams, St. James, and I were kept busy that day treating the stragglers that fell by the roadside. Only half of the regiment marched into camp that night with the Division. One soldier died from sunstroke during the march and was buried at the side of the road near where he fell. About a hundred men straggled into camp all during the night or were brought in by ambulances early in the morning, lack of water being our biggest problem. Unaccustomed as I was to a strenuous march, I myself felt exhausted and sick to my stomach. I was angry, too, at the generals for ordering the men on such a long march during so hot a day through an area of Virginia with such a shortage of water. There was little time or spirit for comradeship, though Adams was civil to all, and to me in particular, through these trying times.

Several days after Ewell had surprised Milroy on June 14 and the latter retreated early the next morning, the rumor finally reached our regiment that Winchester had fallen into Rebel hands. It appeared that the Confederates were moving north right into Maryland and headed possibly for Pennsylvania. What was their objective? Colonel Prescott thought that General Lee wanted to capture Philadelphia. It appeared to me at that moment that Lee should attempt to take Washington if he wanted to win the war. At any rate, it was unsettling that we knew not where the Rebel army was or where they were heading.

On the foggy and overcast morning of June 21 our whole division was sent to support Pleasonton's Cavalry Corps against Stuart's cavalry. The men were eager to finally see some action and have a chance at confronting Confederates. They were very disappointed when our brigade was held back to guard the rear while only Vincent's Brigade was ordered to advance with the cavalry to push Stuart back into Ashby's Gap. Two guns were captured.

The hard days of aimless marching and waiting resumed. We now travelled lighter, with orders coming down for the officers to reduce their baggage. All had to leave behind whatever comforts of life remained. What was the destination and purpose to which our efforts were pointing? All pondered this question with excitement bordering on apprehension.

At 2 a.m. on June 26th the drums started, and soon the regiment was in column on the road. It was our regiment's turn to march at the head of our brigade. We started marching north, the destination being Frederick, Maryland, by forced march.

We crossed the Potomac and entered Maryland on Yankee soil. The road was quite dusty, the sun very hot. We exerted ourselves to keep the patients supplied with water; the water-tanks on the ambulances and the casks on the wagons were kept full at each stop for water. The soldiers well knew to fill their canteens at every opportunity. We medical officers went about recommending frequent rest periods for the men and were often in conflict with the commanders, who were under orders to make certain destinations each day.

Occasionally, a soldier would become over-heated and drop out at the side of the road. Most of these poor sufferers were easy to revive with water and rest, and they were picked up by the ambulance trains following the divisions. Many was the young soldier I held up in a sitting position with one hand as I poured water down a parched throat with the other. I was determined that our regiment would not lose another soul to the heat and forced marches. St. James rode up on his rather large bay mount and looked down on me while I was on the side of the road trying to help one of our fallen boys. He shook his head in disgust and sprayed us with dirt and rocks as he spurred his horse back up to the column of marching soldiers. His exalted position, I supposed bitterly, precluded him from giving a cup of cold water to a lowly enlisted man worn from the rigors of war.

Our brigade of the Fifth Corps arrived near Frederick late Saturday, the 27th, and went into bivouac. The men instantly set about boiling coffee and preparing dinner as they relaxed in anticipation of a few days of rest. That evening more than a few men slipped into town looking for Maryland whiskey, which was plentiful and potent. Not all of these inebriated fellows made it back on their own that night. Many passed out on the streets of town and were picked up the next morning and taken back to their units. The cavalry was kept busy the next few days picking up stragglers from the various corps passing through Frederick on the way north.

That night I sat with a candle on a box trying to write letters to my dearest Mary and the folks at home. The dim, flickering candlelight bothered my tired eyes, and I soon gave up the effort in favor of the morning. I thought of my life back home in Hamilton County. Ah, the contrast now: the carousing, the swearing, the insolence. It had become difficult to control some of the men after days of hard marching. My Baptist upbringing caused me to be alarmed by this sudden lack of respect for authority. Could the regimental commanders of this brigade regain military discipline in time to resume the march north if orders were to suddenly be issued? I worried about the condition of the great Army of the Potomac.

The dawn of Sunday, June 28, was a memorable day for the Fifth Corps. Nothing was planned for that day and the soldiers would be able to recuperate from the long marches, thank God. I had been up most of the night; as the ambulances brought up the stragglers during the night I examined and kept a record on each one for the colonel. As St. James and I prepared to face the long, despondent sick call line that morning, Colonel Prescott came by with startling information.

"General Meade has been named Commander of the Army of the Potomac by President Lincoln effective this very morning," he told us, smiling in a rather unmilitary way. Fighting Joe Hooker was out and would be leaving the Army for Washington that afternoon. The Fifth Corps was honored to have its very own commander appointed to lead the mighty Army of the Potomac as it was about to close with Lee's invading Army of Northern Virginia. "What will this change bring?" " Where is Lee?" were the questions on every lip.

The soldiers in our regiment thought that General Meade would stand up like a man to Lee and fight, but they were not sure that Meade could overcome Lee. The common opinion was that General Meade was a better general than Hooker when it came to fighting, however. Some conceded that Hooker had looked out for his soldiers and had tried to take good care of them.

"We wanted General McClellan to take command again," the soldiers we were tending for weak bowels and summer lung complaints said.

The officers seemed to me guarded about the sudden change of leadership, and well they might have been, while the army was on the march following so formidable an adversary as Lee and the Army of Northern Virginia. At the noon meal Adams told me he thought that a change had been needed, but he felt sorry for General Meade, who would have his hands full the next few days trying to figure out where all of the seven corps were located. Last night when Meade went to bed, he only had to worry about three divisions; now he had seven corps. (General George Sykes had taken over as Commander of the Fifth Corps.)

After the midday meal, Surgeon Adams called us into his tent. He had us sit down on camp chairs. I sensed he was disquieted. St. James and I sat in silence waiting for him to speak. Finally he said that the mail would catch up with us today. Then he said that he particularly missed Boston this time of year, and he was thinking about taking a furlough to go home for a few months. There was another moment of silence as we waited for him to continue. Then Adams said, "I have a feeling that the Thirty-Second is heading into some kind of danger. Call it a premonition that something unfortunate is about to happen to the regiment." After another pause, he said he wanted St. James and me to get the men in the best condition possible for more forced marches and possibly battle. "And if you are praying men I solicit your prayers."

Sunday was a day of rest, ordered by the colonel. The biggest problem was lack of replacements for worn out shoes and socks. Most of sick call that day was for sore feet, blisters, diarrhea, and exhaustion. Their officers told the men to rest as much as they could that day, because painful feet or not, they were going to be on the road north soon. That afternoon mail had indeed arrived for the first time in three weeks, so many of the men had numerous letters to read as they relaxed for the remainder of the day.

I was happy to receive two letters from home. Mother wrote that Father hadn't been able to do much work on the farm because of rheumatism affecting his neck and back. He could barely stand long enough at the pulpit to preach the Lord's word each Sunday. Mother wanted me to consider resigning to return home to help the family work the farm. The family was also in financial straits, so Mother also wanted me to send money home as soon as possible. This would be impossible for some time, because our pay would be late for this month due to the continuous marching. I sighed and put the letter away in the small leather pouch I had for the purpose.

The other letter was from my dear Mary. She thanked me for my five letters. Back home in Indiana they were still talking about the dreary defeat of the Army of the Potomac at Chancellorsville, and there was little confidence remaining in the Union armies in the east. The local citizenry was alarmed, afraid of Morgan the Raider, and the militia was being called out. She reported there was still hope for the Union armies in the West, though. Westerners were more tenacious fighters, she wrote.

Then she mentioned that she had made a trip to Indianapolis in the new buggy of that young lawyer in Noblesville. He was a true gentleman, she went on, and he was earning a considerable amount of money, it was said around town. In fact, he told her he was planning to build a house in downtown Noblesville near the square so that he would be close to the county court house. She obviously felt that he was a nice young gentleman, and I could sense that my dear Mary might be tempted by what he had to offer her. Her letter joined the others in the bundle, and I strolled outside. I had very little to offer Mary at this time. My home was in a tent if a tent was available. I hadn't been paid since I joined the army. I was a nobody, I thought again. Who would blame her if she rejected me? I was worried about my sweetheart, but there was little I could do about it because I was too far away from home.

The next morning was Monday, and activity started slowly. At mid-morning the troops were standing in the rain ready to march. A pontoon train blocked the road north, so we had to wait for the road to clear. By late morning the Fifth Corps was heading northeast away from Frederick, on a sultry day, with the soldiers finding it difficult to march.

I started out marching with the regiment, at the end of the column as usual. My trousers were dirty, as I hadn't been able to wash my clothes for weeks. Each step became uncomfortable, because my trousers rubbed on the numerous boils I had developed on both thighs. After a few hours of marching, I decided to ride in the ambulance for the rest of the day.

Driver Hays was glad to see me, and he offered me some of his chewing tobacco in jest. There were tobacco stains on the seat, but by this time I didn't care. Truly my attitude was gradually changing about my life in general—I could not control anything in it any more, it seemed to me. After a few hours riding in the bumpy ambulance my buttocks were sore again, and this time I could feel that I had a seat sore, to say nothing of the awful boils. I decided to march again with the regiment.

The progress of the corps was limited that day. Tuesday we endured a forced march with the corps, having to cover about twenty-five miles to reach its destination of Union Mills, Maryland. It rained some, making the road muddy. Otherwise, it was so hot and humid that some of the men stepped out of line and vomited at the side of the road, while some others passed out. I attempted to relieve them, but was hard pressed to do so. Straggling was a big problem again, and the following ambulances were filled with the fallen. St. James, on horseback, sneering as usual that these were the weak sisters of the regiment, ordered me to see that they were all picked up by the ambulances so that they would be with the regiment when we arrived at Union Mills.

That night at Union Mills Adams read a circular to us from General Meade's Headquarters announcing that the enemy was moving on the town of Gettysburg in strong force. So our cavalry had finally located Lee. I wondered where Gettysburg was located. Our regiment gave a Union "Huzzah! Retribution for Fredericksburg and Chancellorsville," they shouted. Lieutenant Barrows looked particularly pleased, and clapped me on the back, and I clapped him back, too. That evening General Sykes received orders from General Meade to move north to Hanover the next morning.

We set up the tents that night. After checking the sick stragglers, I tried to get some sleep for the next day's march to Hanover. I put some tepid dressings on my boils. My mind was full of worries and doubts about my future. Was my poor father in pain and anxiety? Then there was my dear Mary. Had her affections settled on another? Though worn out, I fretted and itched and smarted so badly I couldn't get to sleep for an hour.

Wednesday morning was the first day of July. The regiment formed in column in the road with the other regiments of the brigade. The ambulances and the medical supply wagon along with the three other regimental supply wagons waited in a field for the three brigades of the division to march on down the road. While Surgeons Adams and St. James followed on horseback behind the regiment, I had the choice of marching behind the regiment or riding in an ambulance or the medical wagon.

The ambulances, already loaded with footsore and exhausted soldiers, were quite heavy for the horses to pull. My boils had been aggravated by the prolonged marching, so I opted for the medical supply wagon on such a day when I knew the march would be long and the weather oppressive. A huge dust cloud hung over the road where the corps stretched out for many miles. The ambulance train followed the artillery that followed the marching soldiers, and the supply wagons pulled out of the fields onto the road to bring up the rear of the division.

When the wagon train crested a hill top, I had a great view of our mighty corps on the way to Gettysburg. Standing on top of the wagon, I could see for a mile in front and back along the road. As far as the eye could see there seemed to be no end to the columns of moving soldiers, horse-drawn artillery, and trains of ambulances and wagons. And this great corps was only one of seven corps gathering about the enemy that day. We had no idea of where the other corps were located, but we knew they must be out there somewhere doing the same thing we were—marching toward the Army of Northern Virginia. "The Fifth Corps of Lincoln's mighty army has finally come to its moment of trial," Surgeon Adams had prophesied at breakfast this morning. He did not refer further to his premonition, but still

I was a great deal unnerved.

Every now and then when the troops were dragging, the brigade bands and regimental drums would take up the beat, and the men would respond by picking up the pace. As we passed through a village, the flags were unfurled, and the bands played quicksteps. The men stepped lively, I can tell you, when they had an audience of wide-eyed civilians.

The Fifth Corps halted that night just west of Hanover, Pennsylvania, only thirteen miles east of Gettysburg. Having been on the march that day, we received no news of the whereabouts of the enemy or even of the rest of our own army. The men were quick to start boiling coffee, and they looked forward to resting their bleeding, blistered feet and tired bodies.

Our medical unit prepared to receive the stragglers and sick soldiers brought up a few hours later in the ambulances. These men would all need to be examined and a medical report prepared for the colonel, so he would know how many able bodies he could count on for duty. I recall one young private appearing perfectly healthy but suffering from severe nostalgia and fear. He had been picked up by an ambulance when he was found sitting on the side of the road with his head buried in his hands. His musket was missing, and he was sobbing when the stretcher-bearers loaded him onto the ambulance.

I sent for a comrade from his company to take charge of him. Soon I heard, "Ho, Doctor Baldwin." It was Corporal Jacob Phillips, and he spent a long time talking to the man also from the Berkshires. The homesick private revealed that he was tired of the war and no longer wanted to fight. But Corporal Phillips was able to comfort the infantryman and took him back to his company area. I was very impressed by Phillips' ability to talk to this disturbed man and to get him to return to duty. Phillips reminded me of his dream to attend medical school after the war, and I again encouraged him to do so.

Adams, St. James, and I worked late to see that all of the sick and injured soldiers were treated. One soldier had fractured his ankle when he stepped in a ditch. The injured ankle was supported by thin wood side splints confined by a roller bandage. This private and several others with dysentery were sent south by ambulance to be transferred to a general hospital, as they were unable to travel on with the regiment. The soldiers of the regiment retired early for the night to get as much repose as possible in case the morrow brought another long march.

That night a staff officer of Meade's headquarters rode to Hanover to report to General Sykes the situation of the Army. It was then that Sykes and the Fifth Corps first learned the alarming news that there had been a large battle at Gettysburg. This battle involved two Union corps west and north of town. Reynolds' First Corps and Howard's Eleventh Corps had been repulsed, and both corps were swept through Gettysburg onto hills south of town. General Reynolds had been killed that morning. It was uncertain who was in charge of Union troops there tonight, but General Meade was on his way to Gettysburg that very moment.

Adams was very disturbed by the news of Reynolds' death and feared the worst. Colonel Prescott was also deeply affected by this great loss for the army, for he considered Reynolds the best General we had. St. James said that something had gone very wrong this day, and was surprised that we were so far from the rest of the army, which seemed to be scattered over a wide area. Perhaps Meade was not the best choice to take over for General Hooker at this perilous time. I had felt a sickening sense of gloom since hearing the news of the defeat in this little town of Gettysburg, and I could see shock and disbelief on all of the faces of the officers of our regiment. Was Adams' premonition coming true that something dire was about to happen to the Thirty-Second, or even to the entire army? Lee had defeated two of Meade's corps in a single day, and Meade only had five corps left. Was the Fifth Corps next to be destroyed?

The Fifth Corps was ordered to move to Gettysburg without delay. General Sykes immediately notified his division commanders to prepare to move this very night. The weary soldiers were awakened, but the news of battle and the orders to move to Gettysburg immediately that night seemed to impel the men to renewed vigor. I saw some of my footsore patients now, forgetful of their infirmities and ready to join the fight. They wanted Rebel blood. The homesick private, his freckled face red with exertion and excitement, bounded into line next to his comrade, Corporal Phillips. The columns of infantry were formed in the road, and Barnes' Division led the way with Sweitzer's Brigade at the head of the division. I had never seen the

Thirty-Second Massachusetts Regiment so determined. Even the stragglers marched with a fervor that transformed the Thirty-Second into a fighting regiment again.

The moon was eerily bright, and the farms stood out in full relief along the road to Gettysburg. A few families came out to see what was happening and stood by the side of the road in nightdress with their dogs hot and panting at their feet. The tramping of thousands of feet to the beat of drums and the clanking of accouterments mixed with the snorting of horses and mules and the grinding of the wheels of the guns and wagons must have sounded frightening to farm families used to the still of night in the country. They could only guess that something portentous was about to happen somewhere nearby. That clear summer night in July, everyone there was either observing or participating in history, but all would only find that out later.

Sometime after midnight the Fifth Corps stopped five miles east of Gettysburg to rest for a few hours alongside the Hanover Road. News spread rapidly from regiment to regiment of a Union defeat—terrible and humiliating. Some of the men predicted that the Fifth Corps would arrive in time only to witness the Army of the Potomac in flight from Gettysburg. Lee would have yet another stunning victory, and the cause of preserving our beloved nation be placed in further jeopardy. Many ventured the discouraged opinion that this was indeed the beginning of the end.

Rumors flew. General McClellan was now in command of the Army of the Potomac. A large sector of Grant's Army had arrived from the west. Cheers spread down the long line of regiments; the men were believing any piece of hogwash in their enervated state. It was hard to rest, but I lay down, my will heartened by the thought that soon I would surely have my wish to serve as a surgeon.

At 4 a.m. the corps resumed the march west along the Hanover Road and was just east of Gettysburg by 7 a.m. By 10 a.m. the corps had marched south to the Baltimore Pike and went on in to Gettysburg to bivouac just west of the pike. The men immediately started preparing for breakfast as if it would be their last. Adams, St. James, and I were served coffee by Steward Franz, as we prepared for the morning sick call. I was ravenous, but the colonel told us to take sick call first so he could ascertain who was present for duty. The line was quickly formed by the first sergeant, and it was the shortest line I had seen for sick call in weeks. I noted that the freckled homesick soldier was conspicuously absent from the line.

It was Thursday morning, the second day of July.

Chapter IV.

Setting Up The Field Hospital

July 2, 1863

In effect what was occurring on that July 2, 1863 date was that the Army of the Potomac was rapidly concentrating on the high ground south of Gettysburg. Our division had been bivouacked that morning near the Baltimore Pike. The rumor mill still ground on, disgorging various erroneous dreams and flimsy fantasies. The army was planning a retreat to Washington. The army was going to stay and fight it out in this little town. The army was going to have to surrender.

Some of the veterans expressed an uneasy feeling that this would be the confrontation they had both awaited and dreaded—the battle to decide the real fate of both war and nation. That afternoon the division was set in motion in the lower part of Cemetery Ridge near Little Round Top. The Fifth Corps had been ordered to reinforce the Union left flank.

On horseback, Surgeons Adams and St. James led the way for the brigade medical unit assigned to our division field hospital. Our ambulances and medical supply wagons followed close behind the brigade's medical officers, stewards, and hospital detail. The detail included privates assigned to duty as nurses and orderlies from each of the four regiments of our brigade. The musicians from our brigade band were now assigned to the hospital detail.

I noted that two of the drummer boys were younger than my sister Harriet, who was only sixteen years old. In fact, I think they were probably only fourteen years of age because they were much smaller than the rest of the musicians. "They will get in the way and be of no help at best," I said to St. James.

"It's better for them to be detailed to the field hospital, because otherwise they would be with the infantrymen in battle," he told me. Thinking on it, I conceded the wisdom of the statement. Perhaps the man did have some shred of humanity in him after all.

Not having a horse, I chose to ride on the ambulance driven by Jeremiah Hays. He offered me a chew of tobacco. "Take it," he said, "you will need it later." This time I put the grimy plug in my pocket.

The other regimental supply wagons were sent somewhere to the rear with the rest of the Fifth Corps wagon train. Ammunition wagons had been brought up, and the Army was busier than an ant hill. Forty rounds of ammunition had been distributed to each infantryman to fill his cartridge box. The pouches for percussion caps were filled. Rations went into haversacks, and the canteens were topped off with water. I could not help but consider my own sensibilities at this moment of my introduction to the god of war in his fiercest guise. I was fearfully impressed with the gathering of all of these masses of soldiers and weaponry in one place. Sensations of wonder and awe clashed with dread and sorrow for all of the coming death and suffering I knew was inevitable.

I watched Adams on his horse from afar and considered his words. "If you are a praying man, resort to your God now," was the import of what he had stated. It was a moment which would stand out in all of our lives. He was far enough from the bustling streets of Boston and his practice. They all were—the men of this regiment—the fisherman and sailors of Gloucester, from their clapboard houses on winding streets near the salt sea, the Newbury farmers from their sun-drenched, rocky farmsteads with well-kept outbuildings. Far, far away they were from all they held dear on this day of battle.

I looked into their honest countenances and saw the faces of my own former schoolmates in Hamilton County. A Massachusetts man is not really so different from an Indiana lad when it comes to walking into the jaws of death.

Our medical unit set out for the division field hospital soon after the division marched away, advancing to the Taneytown Road and turning south. Progress was slow. When an artillery battery came by, the infantry units marching north in columns of four on this narrow dirt road had to step off of the road quickly to save life and limb. Re-forming on the road, they would march around our ambulances as we worked our way south. The congestion on this road was the worst I had encountered, but it was comforting to see the other corps marching onto Cemetery Ridge. The long days in marching columns had covered all of the soldiers with a fine dust from head to toe, and they resembled spirits of the underworld.

Adams rode beside each ambulance and medical supply wagon to tell the attendants that the house up ahead was to be used as the division field hospital. We were to pull up between the front of the house and the barn. Finally we stopped in front of the large stone farm home on the west side of the Taneytown Road, and I noted with interest the domicile before us, an eight-room house with a large front porch. The house faced south with a lane in front, and south of the lane was a large barn with a small carriage house nearby. A small hill, now known as Little Round Top, stood west of the farm, and south of this hill stood a larger hill, Big Round Top. This was Jacob Weikert's farm, and it had been selected as the division field hospital for both Ayres' Division and ours, Barnes' Division.

A bustle of activity was already underway when we pulled up in front of the house. Ambulances and medical supply wagons were parked all about the farm yard. We went inside and found the kitchen to be a very busy place, with a fire in the stove. Bread was baking, and water was being heated, but the occupants of the house were nowhere to be seen.

Twelve surgeons and about fifty attendants including stewards, enlisted men detailed as nurses and orderlies, and cooks were all hustle-bustle, ready to receive the anticipated wounded. I made the acquaintance of some of the surgeons from Ayres' Division in the house, among them Surgeon John Shaw Billings who was Surgeon-in-Charge of the field hospital for Ayres' Division. He was also one of the operating surgeons for his division. Having made his acquaintance at the Medical College of Ohio in Cincinnati, I was not surprised to see that this energetic man, younger than I by three years and from Switzerland County in the southeastern corner of the state, had become an accomplished military surgeon.

Doors had been pulled from their hinges and placed on boxes and barrels to serve as makeshift operating tables. Stewards were working hard to set out amputation sets and bandages on tables for instant use. Chloroform, tincture of opium, and morphine sulfate solution in glass vials were neatly lined up on the tables. Large tin medicine containers of spirits fermenti were also set out, but had to be guarded as this hospital alcohol was much sought after by some for nonmedical uses.

Our steward, Ludwig Franz, was in the middle of these organizing activities. St. James was very meticulous as he unpacked our surgical instruments and inspected each scalpel, amputating knife, and saw blade for sharpness. Glancing at me, he saw that I was unoccupied, so he showed me the surgical instruments again. Then he produced his own volume of Bernard and Huette's *Illustrated Manual of Operative Surgery and Surgical Anatomy,* with its many illustrations. "Baldy, better get out of the way and study this book while you have a chance. You will soon be needing what's in it." My heart leapt! At last my dream would be realized.

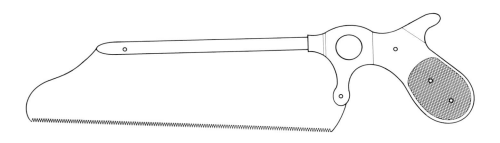

Capital Saw — Satterlee Type

The surgeons assembling in the farm house were nerved but anxious, expecting mass casualties. They traded rumors with each other and spoke as if they knew more about fighting General Lee than any of the Union generals. While the idle surgeons were criticizing the leadership of the Union Army, a group of officers rode up and entered the house. The stewards and orderlies quickly came to attention, but the surgeons, absorbed in their discussion continued to sit about the room. Surgeon Adams, however, recognized one of the generals as the former Commander of the Fifth Corps, and he instantly called for silence and attention, and those surgeons still sitting quickly rose to their feet.

General Meade and his staff were riding the lines to see how the troops were deployed. Most of the surgeons, now aware of what must seem on their part a lack of military courtesy, were flustered and speechless. Surgeon Adams welcomed the commander to one of his Fifth Corps field hospitals. General Meade spoke some pleasantries to the men of his old corps. "I expect every man to do his duty—nothing less."

Then he told them the real reason for his visit to the hospital. The general and his staff had been riding for an hour and were thirsty. They simply wanted some water to quench their thirst; one of the adjutants was outside dipping from the well. Meade had not come to inspect the operating tables or to get advice from the medical officers as to how to defeat Lee. The astute stewards brought in cups of cool well water for the commander and his staff. There was some nervous laughter as General Meade and his party drank their fill of water and promptly continued on their mission.

One story caught my ear that afternoon. I knew of Surgeon Jacob Ebersole from Indiana; he was with the Nineteenth Indiana Regiment in the famous Iron Brigade. The Iron Brigade, along with the entire First Corps, had been decimated the previous afternoon west of Gettysburg, the Confederates having attacked from the west and the north and driven the First and Eleventh Corps through town and up to the cemetery on the hill just south of town.

Surgeon Ebersole had established his field hospital in the railroad depot just north of the town square. He had been treating the Union wounded when the Rebels drove through the town on the heels of the routed Union troops. Ebersole and many of the First and Eleventh Corps surgeons along with thousands of wounded Union soldiers were trapped in town behind enemy lines, so it was said. These surgeons and their medical staff were now prisoners of the victorious Confederate Second and Third Corps, and guards were posted at all of the field hospitals in town. The surgeons had been left alone and continued to treat the wounded from both sides. Chloroform, morphine, and bandages were being depleted because of the overwhelming numbers of wounded men.

But now to the story. Surgeon Ebersole, it would seem, had been able to persuade the Confederates to get word through the Union lines that medical supplies were desperately needed in town. The Union surgeons were trapped in Gettysburg working all night on both Union and Confederate wounded, and so the Rebels were acquiescent and even eager to get medical supplies through to the field hospitals in town. Churches, schoolhouses, barns, and private homes had been commandeered for hospitals for the overwhelming numbers of wounded soldiers from both sides. The Union commanders allowed some medical supplies to be sent into town by ambulance during the night, but the relief mission had to be discontinued after daybreak. It was feared that the captured surgeons and medical personnel would be taken back to Confederate prisons in Virginia.

About 3 p.m. General Barnes received orders to advance his division forward to support Sickles' Third Corps. All of the soldiers of each regiment dropped their knapsacks in a pile on Cemetery Ridge under the guard of one man detailed from each regiment. Sweitzer's Brigade, followed by Tilton's Brigade, marched west to find Sickles' line which was displaced forward of the rest of the Union troops lining Cemetery Ridge. Surgeon Adams, Steward Franz, and I left Assistant Surgeon St. James at the division field hospital. As the two brigades marched west away from Cemetery Ridge, our orders were to join the regiment as surgeons for a dressing station on the actual field itself.

Adams was on horseback with his medical saddlebags fully loaded. I marched on foot at the rear of our regiment with steward Franz and an orderly carrying the medical knapsack on his back. Accompanying us in that location behind the column of infantry was a detail of musicians, drummer boys, and enlisted men to assist as nurses. The brigade tramped and clanked on down the road to find Sickles' line, the ambulances of the brigade following the cadre.

I was frightened to the point of petrification and thought of home with acute yearning. For some reason I had fleeting but pleasant thoughts of Mary and me sitting under a shade tree in the summer time enjoying a Sunday picnic after church. Impending doom shadowed all the faces of the men, even those who were laughing nervously. I suppose I took the prize, because I was the greenest of the greenhorns. The distant roar of cannon and the faint rattle of musketry somewhere off to the left came to our ears like the notes of Gabriel's horn. Men over there were surely getting wounded or even dying this very instant. My legs were rubbery. I became for a moment light-headed. My mouth was dry and my heart was pounding. I wished the elephant or giraffe or whatever it was I had wanted to see were back in Africa and I far away.

Chapter V.

The Dressing Station

July 2, 1863

Sweitzer's Brigade, followed by the men in Tilton's Brigade, was marching west on Wheatfield Road late that afternoon, sometime shortly after 4 p.m., to reinforce the thinly stretched Third Corps line. Against General Meade's wishes, General Sickles had taken his corps forward of the rest of the Union line. Once Sickles was engaged on his left, he was unable to withdraw to the Union line on Cemetery Ridge. And so we units of the Fifth Corps were sent to reinforce his tenuous line.

Dust was thick about the marching feet of the soldiers. The crunch of each step in the regiment, perfectly timed in unison to the beat of a single drum, almost drowned out the distant sounds of battle off to our left. I could see Corporal Phillips just ahead with the homesick private to his right stepping lively.

Lieutenant Barrows had passed me a few moments earlier, courteously but firmly getting the men onto the road. At breakfast I had joshed him about the side whiskers he was growing—a "Burnside" side beard. "You are taking the style of a failed general," I said.

"Let us hope my beard doesn't fail, too," Barrows had retorted with a smile. But he couldn't be more serious at this moment as I observed him bearing the weight of command.

Just a few moments before, I had observed Chaplain O'Mara reminding the men at the end of the column that the Almighty Father in Heaven above required of each soldier to carry out fully his duty and that no one who ran would deserve to go to Heaven. Pshaw. One of the older soldiers immediately handed the chaplain his musket and said, "That goes for you too, Chaplain." Chaplain O'Mara quickly handed back the musket and replied, "Sergeant, I've got something here mightier than the sword," and he held up his tattered Bible for all to see. I became afraid that if we did our duty as the chaplain said—didn't run—and the Confederates did their duty and didn't run—then this would be a very bloody day indeed. But I prayed that I might do my duty also and not play the coward's part and flee the scene.

We passed a wheatfield on our left and then turned south, marching onto a wooded, stony hill just west of the wheatfield. There we halted. Sweitzer's Brigade of a thousand men was positioned in line of battle with Tilton's Brigade nearby on the right. The Thirty-Second Massachusetts Regiment was on the brigade left, and the Sixty-Second Pennsylvania and Fourth Michigan were on the right, the Ninth Massachusetts having been detached for duty elsewhere.

Surgeon Adams ordered us to establish his dressing station behind a group of boulders in the wooded area of the stony hill just northwest of the wheatfield. We set up in a small, flat clearing with large boulders on the north and west sides and several fallen trees on the south side, forming a natural protection for us from stray artillery shelling. The Thirty-Second Massachusetts Regiment was in line of battle only one-hundred yards west of the dressing station.

Steward Franz removed the medical knapsack from the orderly's back and unpacked it on the ground, while Surgeon Adams took his medical saddle bags from his horse and laid them out for ready use. Then Adams had an orderly take his horse back and tie it to one of the ambulances, so the horse could be taken back to the field hospital on the first run. Our three ambulances were parked another one-hundred yards to the rear. Just north of them were parked the rest of the brigade ambulances for the two regiments on our right. A red hospital flag was tied to a lower tree limb nearby to mark the dressing station location and help guide in the wounded. In the midst of the haste and emotion of the moment, Surgeon Adams kindly glanced and nodded at me, giving me reassurance.

I recall being frozen for a moment, listening to the distant rattle of musketry and the thunder of cannon off to the south and west, moving steadily closer. I felt a shiver of panic and fear that set me, truly, a-shaking. I thanked God I wasn't a private in the infantry. The thought of being in line with a musket facing the oncoming enemy and death was more than I cared to dwell upon. I hoped and prayed that these brave infantrymen would hold the line at all cost. The coward in me was starting to show, and as a man of honor, I despised it.

My preoccupation with fear was interrupted by the imperative order to me by Doctor Adams to take the stretcher-bearers forward immediately and place them strategically as instructed. We ran on the double with the stretchers, and I placed the men carrying them at intervals along the line about fifteen yards back. Because of the trees I could see only the adjacent flank of the regiment on our right. But I knew well that tens of thousands of unseen men were on the battlefield around us that day, and my worst fear was that at least half of them were Rebels.

Colonel Prescott had told his officers that our regiment was being sent to reinforce the hard-pressed and unfortunate men of Sickles' Corps. Prescott said that his concern was the fact that the Third Corps was considerably out in front of the rest of Meade's Army and both of Sickles' flanks were in the air and unsupported. We were now as isolated as Sickles, but we had been ordered here to support his line and by no fault of our own. How had Sickles gotten his corps in such a precarious position? Now we had been dragged into the same danger.

For a moment, I stood and looked at a young soldier nearest me, as he looked back at me. He was one of the group that had often come on sick call and was a schoolmate, and from the same hometown as the homesick soldier. His rifle musket was pointed down the slope loaded and at the ready. He could not have been much older than my sister. Was he only sixteen or perhaps seventeen years old? The young soldier slowly turned his head forward as if our eyes had not met. He had apparently learned to submerge fright in duty and action. He continued his surveillance over the ravine to his front as if the first sighting of the enemy was his responsibility and his alone. Some of the older veterans were cool and business-like, but the others seemed extremely apprehensive. Line officers were more animated than usual. Captain Garceau of Company D sharply warned me to get back to the dressing station in the rear.

The dramatic moment was shattered as a stampede of hogs passed in front of our line. Before I could move, the shrill Rebel yell suddenly pierced the woods as butternut-clad soldiers simultaneously appeared in the ravine and came up the slope at us firing. I was petrified, and the only thing that was working was my bladder.

I must have imagined hissing minié balls were immediately to my rear, because I covered the one-hundred yards to the dressing station at a speed beyond my known capabilities.

The musket fire was brisk. A battery of six Napoleons near the crest of the wheatfield to our rear opened up on the Confederates. I could feel the concussion of each blast simultaneously, as the deafening sound reached my ears. To my dying day I will recall the horrible din: the roar of cannon and the constant rattle of musketry mixed with the dreadful Rebel yell and the Union shouts and hurrahs. Our front was now filled with the sulfurous odor of smoke. I could not discern what was happening to our line, and I fully expected to see Rebels running toward us out of the smoke. Shells from someone's artillery were exploding in the tree tops, as leaves and branches were falling all about us. Our line must be holding, because the shouting and cursing continued at a steady rate.

And so the field hospital went into operation. The dressing station had by any sane man's judgment been set up too close to the line, but that was the way Doctor Adams wanted it. Almost unique in the Union forces, Adams deliberately placed his surgeon's field station next to the battlefield. As I helped the few assistants set up the instruments, I realized we were not out of range—I found out what "swifts" were, as an occasional minié ball would whiz by overhead and thud into a tree trunk. I watched Surgeon Adams there on that battlefield as he scanned the rising clouds of gun smoke and kept a keen eye out for the approach of the first of the wounded—steady as a rock.

Soon a few men with minor wounds came walking into the dressing station in different degrees of distress, some cursing and others saying they had flesh wounds. To this day I recall several in detail, perhaps because of the heightened sensibilities of the moment. A minié ball had just grazed the side of one soldier's left forearm, and he demonstrated to everyone that his hand was still able to open and close. He wanted a bandage quickly so he could return to his comrades. Surgeon Adams and Steward Franz were ready and quickly went to work on the wounded man whose sleeve was instantly cut off above his elbow and his wound inspected. The steward poured water on the wound, and Surgeon Adams skillfully placed a pledget of lint shaped to the linear wound and wrapped the forearm with a muslin roller bandage.

The next man was my case, Adams said. A short, stocky soldier half stumbled in, cursing the Rebels and holding his right arm with his left. He was wounded in his right shoulder, with his dark blue blouse stained red and torn at the shoulder. As Steward Franz cut his sleeve off, revealing the entrance and exit wounds to the shoulder, I could see the man could not move his arm. The entrance wound in the front of the shoulder had torn skin edges that were inverted, and the exit wound at the back was considerably larger with everted skin edges and protruding fat. The bleeding was brisk, and I stuffed a wad of lint into each wound and wrapped the shoulder quickly with a muslin bandage roll secured by a pin and a couple of strips of adhesive plaster. The humerus was obviously fractured, so I placed the arm in a sling. Franz gave the brave man an opium pill for pain and a few swallows of whiskey as a stimulant. We instructed him to walk to the ambulance as fast as he could.

By this time the stretcher-bearers, dumping their patients on the ground and running back to the front as fast as they could run, were filling the dressing station. "Be more careful with the wounded," I yelled at one group of stretcher-bearers, but they shouted as they ran for the front that they couldn't take time—fallen soldiers were all over the place. The noise and confusion of battle had taken over, and we surrendered ourselves to meeting the needs of the moment.

Steward Franz seemed to be everywhere, and he was first to check one severely wounded, youthful officer. Franz called for Surgeon Adams to come over immediately. The word quickly spread throughout the dressing station that it was the well-liked Lieutenant Barrows. Several attendants gathered around the stretcher to offer their help to the officer, but it was too late.

Doctor Adams knelt down beside the young lieutenant and quickly determined that he had been killed instantly by a minié ball. His features were already composed in death, and the small fringe of whiskers on his chin made him look especially young and human.

Adams slowly rose to his feet and turned to face the rest of us. Then in an almost inaudible voice with his head down he pointed and instructed us to "carefully carry Lieutenant Barrows over there." The body was taken over to the side of the dressing station and gently rolled off the stretcher onto the ground. The stretcher-bearers paused for just a moment and then quickly ran back to the front lines to pick up another wounded soldier. Adams had tears in his eyes at the personal loss, and I felt sick to my stomach.

Chaplain O'Mara asked Surgeon Adams what he could do to help with the treatment of the wounded. Adams told him "to save all the souls you can, because this afternoon we are going to lose many lives. Comfort the wounded! And assist Doctor Baldwin."

A stretcher was unloaded at my feet. This young soldier boy, pale white, was gasping wildly. The desperate, anxious expression on his face frightened me. I froze and watched him die right in front of my eyes, without an obvious mark on him. I called Adams over. He unbuttoned the dead man's shirt which had a hole in it, and there was a minié ball hole with ragged inverted edges in the boy's chest but with little external blood. Doctor Adams glared at me.

"Doctor Baldwin, as you can see most of the wounded have not yet been treated. Do not waste time on dead men."

"Yes Sir, Doctor Adams," I replied as I tried to calm myself to receive the next wounded man. "But what about the paper pinned to his shirt? I didn't have time to read it. Something about him—"

"That's identification for his body. Don't worry about it now. The burial detail will take care of it."

I looked again at the begrimed face. Freckles showed beneath the battlefield black. It was the homesick boy who had appeared in the sick call line all of the time, Corporal Phillips' friend, who would return no more to his loving home in the Berkshires. Lovely purple-blue mountains, the smell of pine trees clinging to the rocky slopes—but Adams was right; there was no time to even feel regret for him.

The next wounded soldier was carried in shrieking and cursing the stretcher-bearers laboring over the rocky slope. His left leg was flailing over the side of the stretcher and tracing circumduction patterns with each step of the bearers. The thigh had unnatural motion midway up from the knee as the extremity dangled from the stretcher. His light blue trousers were torn at the angulation of the mid thigh with extensive blood stains and bright red blood running down the leg. The patient's pulse was rapid, and he had to be restrained from climbing off of the stretcher. I quickly cut the pant leg of his uniform from the thigh revealing the ragged entrance wound, but I felt around to the other side of the thigh and could find no exit wound.

The poor soldier had a severe femur fracture, and the ball was still in his thigh. He would certainly need prompt surgery at the division field hospital. An orderly applied a tourniquet to arrest the active bleeding, while I applied a pressure dressing and tied the fractured extremity to the other leg. The man was given a few sips of whiskey to counteract the shock and an opium pill for pain. He also begged for water and was given a few sips before being carried to the waiting ambulance. Surgeon Adams hollered to me to remove the tourniquet, but it was too late as the patient was on his way from the dressing station. It could cause gangrene if left on too long. I prayed that someone would have the presence of mind to remove it.

I should pause to note that the proper use of the tourniquet was controversial among military surgeons. The tourniquet was essential during amputation procedures to prevent severe bleeding during the operation, but it was removed at the end of the case. The use of the tourniquet in the field to stop hemorrhage was another issue. Some surgeons felt that many a limb had been lost because the tourniquet had been mistakenly left on for too long, and therefore they considered it the device of the devil.

I turned and there was another severely injured soldier at my feet. The wounded private was from Company D, Captain Garceau's company. Many of the men in this company were from Gloucester, hardy fishermen and sailors, with the reputation of being the best disciplined company in the regiment. I knew this soldier slightly, as he had been detailed to help out in the hospital tent when we were back in Virginia. He had always been particularly helpful to me, but he disliked working around Assistant Surgeon St. James because of the latter's disdainful Boston attitude.

The suffering private was alternately moaning and begging for water. His shirt had been pulled up exposing a nasty abdominal wound with a loop of small bowel poking out. The poor man was also coughing up bloody sputum, and with each cough, the small gut protruded further from the wound. A second large wound was found on the side of his chest. He must have been hit by an artillery shell. One of the drummer boys gave him a sip of water from a canteen, but the water ran out through the chest wound.

I tried to poke the small gut back into the abdominal cavity with my fingers, but it was useless as the intestine just protruded with the next cough. I recall this dreadful scene as if it were yesterday. How warm the abdominal cavity felt to my finger tips. I remember staring at my bloody hands and considering how long to stay there holding in his intestines. I had never felt inside a warm living body, healthy a few minutes ago before the shell fragments struck, certain to be a cold, dead body by tomorrow morning. The orderly nudged me back to reality, and bandages were hastily applied over these mortal wounds of the abdomen and chest and secured with strips of adhesive plaster.

The soldier spoke. "Is the wound mortal?" he whispered. His face registered a mixture of agony and fear. I had him taken to the waiting ambulance without answering his question. Maybe I should have told him the truth then and there. His wounds were obviously fatal, and he knew it from the look on my face. "Mother! Mother!" he cried as they carried him away.

I could hear Chaplain O'Mara saying the Twenty-third Psalm as he walked beside the stretcher, "Yea, though I walk through the valley of the shadow of death, I will fear no evil: for Thou art with me." Mortal wound—I wondered if Doctor Adams would have answered the boy's question then and there. Certainly the surgeons at the division hospital would have to answer that ominous inquiry soon enough.

A youthful private ran to the dressing station shot in the hand, with the bullet having essentially amputated his index finger near the base. The finger was dangling from his hand by a thin remnant of skin. He was told to sit down at the edge of the dressing station to await treatment, but he loudly went about yelling, holding his hand in the air with his finger swinging around limp and blood running down his forearm in a stream.

The youth continued to cry and demanded immediate attention, although everyone was swamped with more seriously wounded men to treat. Finally, to put a stop to the boy's disruptive behavior, Surgeon Adams walked over to where the young soldier was sitting. After examining the powder burns on the hand, Adams told the boy he regretted that his finger would have to come off. The look in Adams' eyes told me he considered this a suspicious injury.

I recall Doctor Adams quickly selecting a scalpel from a small surgical case held by an orderly, and with one swift sweep of the knife, severing the remaining skin completing the amputation of the finger. He threw the amputated finger into the brush and instructed the orderly to bandage the hand and direct the wounded man toward the waiting ambulance. The young soldier looked resigned as his hand was bandaged, but he remained quiet. He seemed reluctant to say anything after that; perhaps it was the case that he had shot himself to avoid further duty. And if so, his silence might mean that a sense of manhood was rousing itself after all.

After some time had passed, the cannon and musket fire faded. We could hear a cheer go up from our line; except for sporadic firing, we seemed in for a lull. This would give us a much needed opportunity to catch up with the backlog of wounded lying on the ground begging for pain medication and water, especially water to assuage the terrible thirst of wounding.

Attendants went around to the waiting men with water and whiskey. The steward distributed opium pills when he was not helping Adams and me bandage wounds. Attendants were holding pressure on bleeding wounds or carrying the deceased off to the side to lie in rows with their dead comrades. Fighting, like a storm crossing the prairie, seemed to be moving far to the left somewhere behind us.

Medical supplies were low, and we were running out of dressings. Clothing was ripped in strips to make bandages. At last one of our ambulances returned with more sorely needed bandages, whiskey, opium, and water. At length the last of the wounded were loaded on the ambulances and on their way to the rear. This gave us a chance to relieve our weary spirits and bodies for a few minutes.

The adjutant galloped up to tell us what we had suspected: the Thirty-Second Massachusetts' line had held in this area, along with the rest of the Brigade including Tilton's Brigade and de Trobriand's Brigade of the Third Corps line. Fighting evidently was continuing far to our left and slightly behind us, with a skirmish line pushed down the slope of the hill into the ravine. The adjutant told us not to leave the area, because it was believed that the Confederates were reforming their lines in the woods. We were not kept in suspense long.

The second Confederate attack started, and the Colonel ordered the skirmish line called in. From my position halfway between the dressing station and the battle line where I was helping a wounded sergeant limp to safety, I could see that the lines were preparing for the Rebel advance. A couple of scared rabbits scampered through our thinned line, as in the distance a long gray line of the enemy appeared through the trees with battle flags flying. As the clink of fixing bayonets resounded from our lines, the Rebel line advanced, yodelling that awful yell and loading on the move. Sulfurous smoke again rose into the tree tops as if the woods were suddenly on fire. I noted nervously that our position seemed more precarious this time, and I felt safer when the limping sergeant and I found refuge behind the boulders of the dressing station. General Barnes ordered his two brigades to fall back to the Wheatfield Road; this they did loading and firing in good order as they crossed to the north side of the road into some woods.

Surgeon Adams was suddenly by my side in this place behind the boulder. The wounded remaining in the dressing station would have to be carried off in a hurry or we would risk capture. He pointed to the Rebel infantry approaching through the trees. It appeared that what I later learned was the Seventh South Carolina Regiment of Kershaw's Brigade was headed right at the dressing station. Surgeon Adams sent me rushing with the stretcher-bearers to get the last of the wounded loaded into the ambulances and order the ambulances to immediately make for the rear. After what seemed like an eternity, I looked back as the last ambulance was starting to move out.

Adams and three men were running from the woods carrying out the last wounded man on a blanket. We halted the ambulance long enough to get this wounded man aboard, then slapped the horses to send them on their way to safety. The Rebels were just starting to come out of the woods.

The Third and Seventh South Carolina regiments stepped out of the woods, stopping to reform their lines at the edge of the clearing. Seeing that we were a medical detail just getting the ambulances away in the nick of time caused them to gallantly cheer us and wave their hats in the air. These intrepid, gray-clad troops obviously were holding their fire to give us the opportunity to reach safety. They could easily have cut us down like a scythe through wheat if they had wanted to do so. I had never seen anyone from South Carolina before, and now I was observing at fairly close hand hundreds of its sons. The cruel war that was tearing us apart was at the same time bringing us together in a peculiar, wrenching way. We ran like fiends from hell across an open field to catch up with our regiment, which was crossing the road to the north and entering the woods there. I was completely out of breath on reaching the safety of the trees. As I looked eastward up the road to see the last ambulance disappear in the distance, an exhausted but smiling Adams handed me the red hospital flag he had saved. It had been shot full of holes.

Sweitzer's Brigade watched from these woods as Meade sent in more reinforcements in an attempt to save Sickles' Third Corps from being overrun by Longstreet's massive assault. Caldwell's Division of four brigades came through the woods from their Second Corps position on Cemetery Ridge and crossed the road on their way to the wheatfield. As soon as they arrived at the wheatfield, these four brigades were sent in by General Caldwell. Cross's Brigade went in first, advancing south across the eastern part of the wheatfield. Zook's Brigade went in next, advancing west to stony hill. We watched the famous Irish Brigade enter the field and quickly form in line of battle with their muskets and fixed bayonets on their right shoulders. Kelly green flags, side-by-side with the Stars and Stripes, floated proudly over the line as the Irish cheered and stepped off to begin their charge on Zook's left. Finally, Brooke's Brigade advanced across the wheatfield southwest into the woods. The brave charges of Caldwell's Division swept the Rebels from the field, a sight I would never forget.

Sweitzer's Brigade was ordered by General Barnes to support Caldwell's Division. We watched the three regiments enter the wheatfield where they were exposed in the open. The Thirty-Second Massachusetts marched in on the left, the Sixty-Second Pennsylvania was in the center, and the Fourth Michigan formed on the right. Surgeon Adams led our medical detail into the field immediately behind the lines and then ordered us to stop. Looking around I saw a cluster of ten dead artillery horses. They lay in distorted positions near the site where Winslow's Battery of six Napoleons positioned on the higher ground at the wheatfield's crest had lent much support and comfort to the infantry an hour before. But now Winslow's guns were gone, and the brigade would have to go forward alone without artillery support. The brigade advanced in line of battle across the wheatfield nearly to the stone wall on the southwest corner of the field.

The wheat had been almost totally trampled down by the human waves of infantry passing back and forth across this field of death. Completely littering the open field were the dead and wounded from both sides, intermingled. The walking wounded were helping each other in pairs and groups to make their way slowly eastward toward the main Union line.

The sound of the painful groans and cries of the downed men coming from all directions on the field would have melted the hardest heart. As the brigade passed by them, the afflicted soldiers called out for help, but unfortunately no one could aid them. Stretcher-bearers, following behind the brigade, had orders to stay with their respective regiments, so they could not stop to pick up the numerous wounded men already on the ground.

Surgeon Adams ordered us to quickly set up our dressing station anew at the upper end of the wheatfield. We were behind the stone wall, along the far eastern border of the field near the Wheatfield Road. Adams sent the ambulances further east along the road to await his orders. From this new vantage point we could only see the eastern half of the wheatfield; our brigade was mostly out of sight at the lower western extreme of the field. The rattle of musketry coming from Rose's woods southwest of the wheatfield told us action was underway, however. When the wounded men arrived, we would call for the ambulance train to come forward. Adams and I waited for the stretcher-bearers to bring in the wounded.

Soon Rebel bullets, coming from Rose's woods, began peppering the Thirty-Second Massachusetts in the center and left flank. From Rose's woods the Sixty-Second Pennsylvania and the Fourth Michigan were being shot at, and their right flank was hit by bullets coming from the woods of stony hill. The three regiments seemed to be facing the wrong way; the enemy had flanked them on the right. But as soon as the regiments turned around to face the new fire, they found they were nearly surrounded. Colonel Prescott was wounded and escorted to the rear, and Lieutenant Colonel Stephenson took command of the Thirty-Second.

Although we at the dressing station did not fully understand the action, what was occurring was that the Confederates of Anderson's, Semmes's, and Kershaw's brigades had charged from the woods from all directions with fixed bayonets. Fighting was at close quarters with musket and pistol fire, sword, bayonet, clubbed muskets, and fists. The brigade started falling back under the overwhelming Rebel force coming from three sides. The Fourth Michigan was pushed back into the Sixty-Second Pennsylvania. Colonel Sweitzer's horse was shot out from under him. As the Thirty-Second Massachusetts was falling back, our frustrated Colonel Sweitzer ordered the regiment to halt their retreat and turn around to stand their ground. Lieutenant Colonel Stephenson ordered the Thirty-Second to face forward and fire. The Confederates then concentrated their fire on our regiment, Stephenson was shot in the face, and the situation grew desperate. As the three regiments retreated as best they could, east away from the wheatfield, Sweitzer's Brigade was shot to pieces . Most of the wounded were left where they fell in the wheatfield. Only a few of the walking wounded could be helped off of the field by their comrades, and they stepped over the stone wall and began coming in at this moment to the dressing station for treatment.

These wounded men were made to lie down behind the stone wall for shelter from the stray bullets. Adams, Steward Franz and I applied bandages as fast as we could. We started any wounded man who could walk up the road to the rear. The stretcher-bearers with the brigade had suffered casualties and run from the field just before the entire brigade line gave way. We worked a while in this hot situation; actually I was in the midst of applying pressure to a hemorrhaging thigh wound when I heard Surgeon Adams ordering the dressing station to pack up again! The heat of the battle necessitated that we pull back to the east to the Union line on Cemetery Ridge just north of Little Round Top.

Just as I finished applying a tight dressing on the thigh to stop the bleeding, Adams told me to run up the road to send the ambulance train to safety. I ordered the ambulances into a field to turn around and sent them up the road to the rear behind Union lines on Cemetery Ridge. The seriously wounded in the dressing station were given sips of whiskey, opium pills, and canteens of water as we prepared to abandon them to the mercy of the victorious Rebels. We took care of a few of the Confederate wounded, and we expected no less honorable treatment from them in caring for our wounded.

Union soldiers from the Second, Third, and Fifth Corps were mixed together, having streamed east over the stone wall at the eastern end of the wheatfield after the collapse of the entire Union left flank. At the last possible moment Surgeon Adams gave us the final order to abandon this dressing station at the stone wall, and he sent Chaplain O'Mara out of harm's way to the field hospital at the Weikert farmhouse to help Assistant Surgeon St. James.

By this time I could see the approaching Confederate lines coming up the gradual slope of the eastern half of the wheatfield, and there were no Union regiments left between the enemy and the dressing station at the stone wall. Quickly we helped the walking wounded to escape to Cemetery Ridge. Surgeon Adams and I finally said farewell to the brave but seriously wounded soldiers we had to leave behind at the stone wall, and then we ran with Franz for the main Union line.

Sickles' precarious blue line had been broken by the Confederates and was being swept from the field by Longstreet's assault. The wheatfield was soon completely in Rebel hands, and this rout of major proportions was a terrible defeat for the Union.

Sweitzer's Brigade retired for the day just north of Little Round Top on Cemetery Ridge. Only about fifty exhausted men and officers assembled that night with the regiment. Surgeon Adams, Steward Franz, and I were present to treat any minor wounds or injuries. We had treated more than sixty wounded men that afternoon.

The battle was over for the Thirty-Second Massachusetts. Our regimental losses were later estimated at about eighty killed and wounded for the engagement from a regiment that went into battle with 227 men and officers. How many were left out in the wheatfield was at that time unknown. Men were scattered about on Cemetery Ridge and Little Round Top and would, we hoped, find our camp during the night or in the morning. How many were captured in the wheatfield was also unknown. Corporal Phillips was missing.

Around the campfire, as we tried to cook and eat a few mouthfuls in the midst of almost total exhaustion, I heard someone say that this had been a disaster of unprecedented proportions for the regiment and the brigade. If our section of the battle was any indication, the general opinion was that Meade was certainly finished. Certainly the Thirty-Second Massachusetts was finished as an effective fighting unit for the time being.

I sat there staring dully into the fire, stunned by what I considered to be yet another unbelievable crushing defeat of the Union forces at the hands of the Confederates, the second straight day of defeat for the Army of the Potomac. (We did not, of course, have knowledge at that time of the Confederates' failure to win decisively that night.) I had dark thoughts that the United States was finished as of this very night. We would probably pull back toward Washington in the morning. Gloom possessed me, and I asked bitter questions of myself. Where were these people I had read about in the Hoosier newspapers, who could experience war and like it? Where was the glory? What, indeed did that word mean? I confess that at that moment, looking at the broken fragments of what had once been a fine regiment, I had not the slightest idea.

As I lay there on the ground, the faces of the men I had treated all of this day, a day that seemed to last a thousand years, came before my eyes—the homesick soldier, the likable Lieutenant Barrows. I could see a case made to justify the horrendous slaughter if we had won, but no, dismal, humiliating defeat was our portion.

Then I looked up. Surgeon Adams had busied himself by examining a few of the men with minor wounds and injuries. He seemed not to be worried about the condition of the army or defeat of the United States. He looked down at me. He must have seen the pain in my eyes. "So many wounded, so many dead in the wheatfield," I said. "Your premonition came true."

"So it did," he said. "But now that battle is over, and we face another. It will be another opportunity."

I shook my head. The futility of it all was overwhelming.

"You did your duty and did it well. Focus on the condition of the regiment," he said. "The men of the regiment are talkative and in good spirits. They are proud of the fine showing of the regiment this day. They are not defeated men." He was right. I looked around me. The remnant, whoever they were, were laughing, joking, and playing cards.

Then Doctor Adams announced to me that it was time for us to report to the division field hospital. We left Steward Franz in charge of any medical problems in the camp and returned to the Weikert farmhouse to help out with the masses of wounded accumulating there. It was after sundown, and there would be no sleep tonight for any of the medical staff.

Chapter VI.

The Division Field Hospital

July 2, 1863

It was dark by the time Surgeon Adams and I arrived at the Weikert farmhouse, now being used as a field hospital not only by two of our divisions, but by surgeons from the Second and Third Corps as well. We saw the bodies of two field officers and that of a lieutenant of artillery lying together on the front porch. They were said to have been mortally wounded on Little Round Top. As I paused to look around the porch, the dim flickering light of a nearby lantern fell on the face of the dead artillery lieutenant. He looked familiar, but I could not just then place where I might have seen him. Then a private standing on the porch observed me staring at the corpse, and the private solved the mystery by supplying the man's name, "Hazlett, sir. Shot through the head." Then for a brief moment I recalled seeing the broken Parrott gun blocking the road and talking to Lieutenant Hazlett during repairs. The shock of this revelation was short-lived because I was becoming numb to personal tragedy. My outlook on life had been changed in just one afternoon.

We cautiously entered the dark house, which was already filled with the wounded. One had to be careful to step around the many patients scattered about the floor, some moaning, some screaming, and others forever silenced by the grim, gray wing of the angel of death. The activity level had reached a frenzied pace. Surgeons hovered around the numerous makeshift operating tables performing various surgical procedures under flickering candle light.

The smell of chloroform permeated the house. All of the windows were wide open for ventilation, and gnats were swarming about the candle light. The small tables about the rooms were completely covered with surgical instruments and rolls of muslin bandages, and long amputation knives and bone saws with their handles protruding sat in pans of bloody water, ready to be grabbed by the busy surgeons. Orderlies and attendants were amazingly efficient in the dispatch of their duties, toting and carrying human cargo as if they were dockhands. They bore the wounded men into the house and took the treated and dead out to the yard and barn.

Surgeon Adams and I located Assistant Surgeon St. James working in the corner of the dining room on one of the three tables crowded into that small room for surgery and staffed by surgeons from our division. In spite of weariness, my spirits rose. I was at last getting the opportunity to see and assist with real surgery. I had heard that learning a surgical procedure was "see one, do one, teach one." My heart was pounding at this opportunity to "do one."

O'Mara circulated quietly among the fallen, saving souls now, whereas a moment before he had been helping St. James save lives. Chaplain O'Mara had been giving the chloroform for the patients on Teddy's surgical table until Doctor Adams took over for the anesthesia, freeing him for the task of the many prayers he would need to say tonight. Adams instructed me to assist St. James with the surgery

Soon in the dim candle light a screaming soldier was placed on our table. An orderly had cut the man's shirt sleeve off at the shoulder. Teddy quickly looked at the man. "Gun shot wound to his right elbow," he said. "It's shattered the humerus at the elbow joint." Amputation was needed immediately. The man could move his fingers and almost make a fist. If the situation were not so desperate and pressing, consideration could have been given to excision of bone at the joint and salvage of a flail but otherwise intact limb with a functioning hand. These were limited, emergency conditions. That night this injured young soldier would get an amputation.

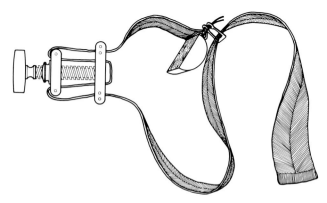

Tourniquet

Adams began by pouring the chloroform upon a handkerchief folded into the shape of a cup. He instructed the terrified patient to take slow, deep breaths and gradually brought the handkerchief closer to the man's mouth and nose. Soon the handkerchief was only a half inch from the patient's face. Suddenly the frightened soldier yelled, "Don't cut my arm off; please don't cut my arm off." Adams poured more fluid on the handkerchief and in about five minutes the struggling man was only able to whimper.

Now, at last, my moment had come. I was to assist in an amputation.

"Do just as I say," St. James commanded sharply. I applied the tourniquet as high up the arm as possible and tightened it. An attendant secured the forearm while I held the upper arm. St. James reached for a long Catling amputating knife sharp on both edges, with a sharp point on the end. Before I knew what was happening, he plunged the knife through the center of the arm midway between the elbow and the shoulder. He cut a flap of tissue from inside out on the front of the upper arm. The wounded soldier's fingers quivered as the sharp knife stimulated and divided the nerves in the arm. Just as quickly St. James cut the back flap and told me to grab the bloody flaps with my fingers and pull them up the arm. The humerus was then widely exposed, and he quickly scraped the remaining soft tissues from the bone.

Turning around quickly, St. James grabbed the capital bone saw. He cut the humerus with rapid saw strokes. The anesthesia must have been a bit light, for the patient mumbled during the time of the saw cut. As soon as the bone had been divided, the limb was free. Teddy threw the amputated arm out the open window. We ignored the swear words that drifted back in through the window; in passing I noted that some sergeant outside was probably shaking his fist at us while attempting to wipe the blood from his blouse.

I continued to retract the skin flaps while St. James hooked the brachial artery with a tenaculum and ligated it with silk thread. He instructed me to release the tourniquet. Immediately the large surgical wound filled with the ooze of bright red blood, and the ligated artery pulsed with each heartbeat. A troublesome bleeding vein required ligature, so I again retracted the bloody flaps with my fingers while he tied off the vein with silk thread. The thread ends of the ligatures were brought out of one corner of the wound. St. James explained that the thread would come away from the artery spontaneously in about ten to eighteen days. The surgeon could give it a tug at that time to help separate the ligature from the artery, but there was some danger of secondary hemorrhage. He sponged the bleeding muscle to remove the clots and blood, and the small bleeders were controlled with pressure. In a few minutes the flaps had been approximated with several widely spaced silk sutures. Adhesive straps were placed on the skin between the sutures.

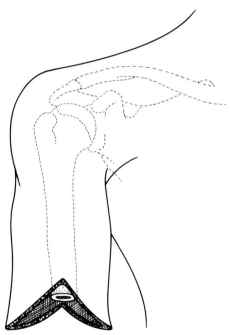

Amputation Through Humerus

The dressing was applied by placing a pad of folded flannel over the surgical wound and wrapping a muslin bandage roll over this pad and about the amputation stump and upper arm. Adams let the patient awaken from the anesthesia while the bandage was being applied. "When are you going to cut off my arm?" the groggy soldier asked. An orderly helped the bewildered man up from the table and led him into the next room to lie down and wait his turn to be carried out to the barn. A few sips of water and whiskey were given to comfort him, but this show of kindness caused the man to retch and finally vomit on the front of his shirt. Wiping my bloody hand on my apron, I sighed. This would be a long night for everyone.

The next wounded soldier placed on the table was gritting his teeth but moaning very little. This truly brave man had a single minié ball wound in the front of his thigh. Bullet wounds on the back side can sometimes raise questions as to which way a man was facing during the battle, although of course, bullets can come from both directions at once. The trousers had already been cut from the extremity, and there was no exit wound. I watched the assistant surgeon examine the thigh and instruct the soldier to try to lift his leg off of the table. This he could barely do with a great deal of effort and pain. "The femur has not been broken by the ball," St. James said and Adams nodded. This patient had a chance for a good recovery.

St. James suddenly stuck his right index finger deep into the thigh wound to explore it for the bullet, with the result that the patient immediately let out a terrifying series of yelps. I held him down with the help of two orderlies. St. James commented that he could just feel the bullet at the tip of his finger. He took the bullet forceps and was able to grab the conical lead ball, but it could not be pulled out past the tight skin about the entrance wound.

He picked up a scalpel and made a single slit in the side of the wound, causing the patient to buck on the table in a fierce struggle with the two attendants and me. St. James again took up the forceps and this time was successful in removing the conical ball, but in the process he stirred up some brisk bleeding. As I tried to calm the wounded man following his very painful surprise, the stewards applied pressure to the bleeding hole.

St. James stuffed wet lint into the wound to stop the bleeding, and pressure was maintained on the wound by wrapping a muslin bandage roll around the thigh. I hoped someone in the barn would check this bandage in a few hours to be sure it was not too tight. The cursing patient was carried from the room. He gave us a look that could kill. Some chloroform would have been helpful while they were extracting the bullet, I told myself.

The chief ambulance officer for the Fifth Corps came into the house. "There will be an informal truce tonight with the Rebels until 4 a.m. for purposes of bringing in the wounded soldiers left on the field of battle," he announced. He wanted to recruit a few assistant surgeons to accompany him on a mission of mercy.

"You go, Baldwin," Surgeon Adams said, waving me away as he prepared for another amputation.

There were about eighty ambulances and crews out that moonlit night searching for our wounded men in the wheatfield. Of course, we would bring in all wounded whether friend or foe.

I can safely say it was the eeriest, most agonizing hour of my life. The moonlight was bright enough to reveal ghost-like human forms on the ground, but in the odd illumination, it was often hard to tell who was dead or alive. I thought how different this would look in the daylight. Colors were difficult to distinguish in the moonlight, and shadows distorted the figures into gruesome forms. It was difficult to distinguish who belonged to which army, what with the Confederate wounded intermingled with ours. Probably it did not matter.

Ambulance Wagon

Many of the stretcher-bearers were accustomed to kicking the bodies to see if life yet existed in them. I decided I would identify the survivors as expeditiously as possible and have the stewards and orderlies dress their wounds while I directed the stretcher-bearers to those ready to be loaded on the ambulances. While waiting to be picked up, the wounded soldiers were offered whiskey and water. All over the field wounded soldiers were calling out to us for help, many begging for water to quench their terrible thirst. The dead and dying covered the entire wheatfield area.

The stretcher-bearers conveyed the wounded soldiers to the ambulances as fast as was humanly possible. Initially some of the wounded Confederates were left behind on the ground by a few of the ambulance crews, but the ambulance corps officers and surgeons gave instructions that all of the Rebel wounded were to be picked up also. A few Confederate surgeons and stretcher-bearers were in the same area and spoke to us. They had limited means to recover their wounded. "Please," one bearded gray-clad man called to me, "Please fellow, would you all pick up our men? We face the choice of leaving them." The Rebels were courteous and well spoken. Stretcher-bearers of both sides conversed together as they worked and sometimes helped each other. Those who are committed to giving aid to the gravely ill do not look at uniform color or insignia, after all. The singular camaraderie of that night would change after 4 a.m. We had strict orders to leave the area by that time or risk life and limb.

At the lower west end of the wheatfield, one Rebel was singing a hymn to try to calm and comfort the wounded soldiers of both sides. "Abide with me/Fast falls the eventide; The darkness deepens/ Lord, with me abide; When other helpers fail and comforts flee/ Help of the helpless, oh, abide with me." I can still hear that strong baritone voice ringing over the clearing in the misty moonlight, comforting those of both North and South. I myself felt God's presence there in that terrible, bloody field. I met no atheists in the wheatfield that night.

I plodded on across the wheatfield trying to finish the first sweep as soon as possible. Empty ambulances were brought the minute the loaded ambulances had been sent on their way to the field hospitals. It seemed to take forever to reach the stone wall and woods on the south side of the field.

I was dismayed by the slowness of our mission. We turned north and started our second sweep across the wheatfield further west on down the slope. As we started back across the field, the sight of the lines of ambulances coming onto the field and leaving the field inspired me with renewed energy. Patience and persistence, truly of all the virtues, were most needed that night in the wheatfield.

One serious accident occurred that night. I saw a loaded ambulance moving north across the slope of the wheatfield, when the front wheel on the upper side of the slope hit a large rock. The ambulance slowly rolled over, spilling its human cargo out and pulling one horse to the ground. There were terrible screams of pain from the wounded men, mixed with the cries of the ambulance crew calling for help and the neighing and scrambling of the startled horses. Another ambulance came up to take the twice wounded men from the field.

As I recall it, the wrecked ambulance had a broken axle. When the two horses were cut loose, one ran away into the darkness. The other fallen horse had a broken leg and had managed to get back up. There he was hobbling around on three legs until an officer walked up and put his revolver to the horse's head. The poor beast fell into the wheat and rolled onto one side. After the legs twitched several times, he lay still. We left the ambulance on its side, abandoning it to the world of the dead in the wheatfield.

On our third sweep, as we approached the south edge of the field farther on down the slope, we heard a frantic cry for help coming from deep in the woods. An ambulance corps officer and I ran across the field, jumped the low stone wall, and plunged into the woods toward the source of the sound. Following the cries, we entered a small clearing. I saw in the moonlight a pack of snorting swine tearing at human bodies. Only one wounded soldier remained alive in the clearing, and he was quite naturally screaming in absolute terror.

I went in first kicking at the snorting hogs, but they refused to leave their feast. One of the beasts spun around, knocking my feet out from under me. Instantly I was on the ground next to a partially eaten corpse. The line officer had come in right behind me and drew his sword, running a couple of hogs through with the tip. Swine are apparently smarter than men; they left the area after only two of their own went down. They would be back to finish their meal, as soon as we were gone.

As I knelt down to examine the wounded man, he surprised me by calling out my name. "Doctor Baldwin, is that you?" I assured him that it was. His face was so blackened by dirt and powder that I did not recognize him at first in the moonlight. "You came to get me, didn't ya? I knowed you would, 'cause we're from the Thirty-Second, ain't we?"

It was Corporal Jacob Phillips, who had been missing in action since this afternoon. "Where are you hurt, Jacob?" I asked. He pointed to his right leg. His shoe and sock were caked with dry blood, and his foot was twisted off to the side. He explained that some Rebels had chased him into the woods, and in trying to escape, he severely twisted his ankle. The Rebels caught him and were threatening to run him through with the bayonet, but as he cried out for mercy, pleading his serious injury, they decided to spare his life. On pulling down his sock, I could see that he had a severe ankle fracture with the end of the tibia sticking out of the skin.

I told Phillips that we had to carry him out of there and that it would be painful. He cried out, though he tried not to, as we carried him from the woods to the edge of the wheatfield and called for assistance. Soon his ankle was bandaged and splinted with a board, and he was loaded safely into an ambulance. I gave him whiskey and sips of water and assured him, "I'll see you at the hospital, Jacob." We could hear the snorting and the rooting of the hogs back in the woods, but we could not stay to protect the dead from being eaten that night.

The informal truce in the wheatfield was running out. The ambulances had to be sent back to the rear. Sadly, I realized we surely had missed some of the wounded who were unconscious and couldn't get our attention, the ones who would most likely die anyway. But we could feel a sense of gratification. The ambulance system had been tested severely tonight, and I can testify that it was working well at Gettysburg. In fact it seemed that the entire medical department was being tested severely tonight, and I hoped that the medical staff might do as well as the ambulance corps did in the wheatfield. A little more than a thousand wounded had been transported to the field hospitals from the wheatfield alone. It was a triumph for the organization of the ambulance corps, and I wish to pay tribute due at this time.

I arrived back to the Weikert house just as the rosy streaks of dawn were starting to show in the east. The hospital was about as I had left it the night before, except that the yard around the house was full of wounded men lying on the cold ground. The barn was also completely filled with the wounded. In the early light of the new day, I could see wounded Confederates lying in the yard with our men. These wounded Rebels lying unguarded here were our wounded now.

I circled the house to get the lay of the land. East of the house on the other side of the Taneytown Road was a pile of arms, hands, legs, and feet forming a pyramid half as high as the fence. A tired orderly from the house crossed the road and stopped at the pile of amputated limbs. He was carrying some legs and arms and threw them on the pile like freshly cut cord wood. Two tattered Rebels were picking through the pile. Something prompted me to walk over to help. "What are you doing you filthy traitors?" the orderly was demanding.

"Seekin' Billy's arm," they replied without looking up. "He's taken a fancy to havin' his arm back for a proper burial." I tried to help them for a few minutes, but I soon realized the fruitlessness of the task; they had no idea which arm belonged to their friend.

On entering the house, I found Doctors Adams and St. James in the dining room, where I had last seen them. They were amputating the leg of a young soldier below the knee. We were all past being tired, having not slept for more than twenty-four hours, but there would be no sleeping until the last wounded man had been treated, or until we dropped senseless in our tracks.

Chapter VII.

Move To The Fifth Corps Field Hospital
July 3, 1863

At the Weikert farmhouse the wounded had been unloaded from ambulances in the front yard. All night the surgeons had worked over six tables set up in the house, and the attendants carried the wounded soldiers in and out of the house in a constant stream. The early morning sunlight seemed unnaturally bright; its glare fully revealed the impact of the fighting from the previous day on the Union left.

I went to work holding limbs while surgeons Adams and St. James removed them. After two hours of this, I stepped out on the front porch of the house for some morning fresh air. I recall that the birds were in the trees singing their songs, oblivious to all the human misery down below on the ground. I sat on the ground, and for a few brief moments I slept, in spite of myself. When I awakened two surgeons were working in the yard with a group of stewards and male nurses to try to sort out the patients by severity of the wounds. They were attempting to impose some organization on what was essentially a chaotic situation.

The Union wounded from the Second, Third, and Fifth corps were lined up randomly in rows on the ground along with wounded Confederates. The mortally wounded were being carried off to the far side of the yard to die. Musicians from the brigade bands were detailed over there to comfort these dying soldiers by offering them water for their severe thirst and seeing that they had straw and blankets on which to lie.

Those soldiers with minor injuries had their wounds bandaged by the dressing surgeons, and then they were taken away to the back yard, because the barn was completely filled. The remaining, seriously wounded soldiers would have to wait their turn to be taken into the farmhouse for treatment by the operating surgeons, Confederate wounded treated equally with Yankee.

I walked around the house again to stretch my legs before going inside. I had never dreamt there could be so much human misery in one place at one time. The barn housed several long rows of bandaged men lying on straw and completely filling the barn from wall to wall. Continuing around the house to the east side, I saw rows of Union dead side by side in the field across the Taneytown Road. The pile of amputated limbs had now reached the top of the fence.

I walked rather wearily back to the front of the house. Some batteries of the artillery reserve were headed north on the Taneytown Road, kicking up the usual dust cloud. I wondered if the fighting would be serious again today, and I hoped the Thirty-Second Massachusetts could remain in a reserve position because of its terrible losses yesterday. Far off to the north I could hear the rumble of artillery. The Union right flank seemed to be feeling the action this morning.

I entered the house and went to the kitchen for a cup of coffee. There was a large open box of hardtack—breakfast, dinner, and supper. The coffee was strong and full of grounds, but I relished it, as one always does simple things in time of heightened anxiety. Surgeon Adams nodded to me as I stood holding my cup. Some of the surgeons were congregating in the kitchen to boast about the large numbers of amputations that were done and trade war stories of the unusual cases they had operated on during the night.

I listened. A surgeon could get more experience here in one night than he could get back home in years. Some of the surgeons were comparing amputation scores. In a few days they could more relevantly keep score of how many had died after surgery, but I doubted most of them would ever know. Armies move after battles, and the surgeons move with them.

There was talk also of the progress of the battle. The Rebels had routed the Union forces two days ago, and sadly, it appeared we had not turned them back yesterday. Rumor had it that General Meade decided last night to keep this Army here. We speculated as to what Lee might do, and we expected him to attack again—he was a very aggressive commander. We wondered what Meade had planned for the day, but we doubted that he would hazard an attack on Lee. Would we have another humiliating defeat for the Union to add to Chancellorsville and Fredericksburg?

Adams had returned to the dining room, and he and St. James were again at work at the surgical table. They were ready to have the next patient put to sleep, so they gave me the index finger down sign to start administering the chloroform. The table was covered with layers of dry blood, and the floor had so much blood on it by this time that straw was brought in to cover and soak it up. Scattered about the room were pans filled with bloody water and instruments. Flies congregated in black clouds all over everything. It was a hopeless task to try to swat them away. Occasionally a surgeon would holler for an orderly to change the water in his pan so the amputating knives and saws could be rinsed of the blood.

With the incessant surgery, the knives were growing dull, and it became difficult to cleanly cut through the soft tissues. Adams selected one orderly to keep busy all the time sharpening the long amputating knives. All of the medical staff, stewards, nurses, and orderlies looked haggard, worn, and dull. But few in the Medical Department at Gettysburg were sleeping this morning.

For awhile I administered chloroform for Adams and St. James. Through the window I could watch the army cooks outside in the yard working frantically around the clock over open fires to try to keep up with the need for nourishment for the wounded soldiers. Even the supply of fresh water from the well was starting to become scarce and had to be rationed. It was obvious at that point that the medical system was hopelessly overwhelmed, the supplies mostly exhausted. The supply wagons were expected at any moment, and we all prayed to catch sight of them soon.

When the chief surgeon of the Fifth Corps came in a short while to tour the Weikert farmhouse to oversee the care of the wounded soldiers, he confirmed that the situation of the food, water, and medical supplies was indeed grim. He determined that the supply wagons just now coming up would be inadequate for the large number of casualties.

I must have appeared inactive at the time, as he grabbed my arm and told me he had an important job for me. I was to take his horse and ride immediately to the telegraph tent to send an urgent message to ask the Medical Department at Washington for more emergency supplies, to tell them the medical situation was grave and expected to get much worse today. The helpful Sanitary Commission would, of course, be headed here by now as the news of Gettysburg had been carried far and wide by the newspapers, but they would be only a small part of the solution. Systematized assistance was called for, and called for now.

He took pencil and paper from his pocket and quickly wrote out the terse message. Within minutes I arrived at the telegraph tent, located just north up the Taneytown Road from our hospital. A line of newspaper journalists lounged in front of the tent. I had expected I would just walk up to the front of the line and have the telegraph operator send off my priority message for medical help. The telegraph operator, however, was quite occupied, it seemed, and waved me off to the end of the line. The journalists laughed, and they railed at me for trying to cut in line in front of them. Each reporter's message seemed to be quite important and lengthy, I noticed, and the system seemed to dictate that they pay the telegraph operator a gratuity on the sly. I began to feel apprehensive. The line was not moving at all.

A solution presented itself. I had noticed that infantry staff officers came and went at will and would cut right in and get their messages sent out immediately, so I grabbed the next staff officer as he left the telegraph tent. I explained, "I have an urgent message from the chief surgeon of the Fifth Corps for medical supplies." The lieutenant colonel was on General Meade's headquarters staff and very sensitive about what happened to the wounded infantry soldiers. He walked rapidly up to the telegraph table and firmly said, "Send this message to the Medical Department in Washington immediately." The operator was busy sending out a news story for one of the reporters standing next to the table. He was tapping out the code on the telegraph key as he yelled indifferently, "Take this man to the end of the line. He'll have to wait his turn."

But the lieutenant colonel was not to be dismissed in such urgent circumstances. He stood erect behind the telegraph operator and faced the line of impatient journalists taunting me for again trying to cut in ahead of them. The staff officer drew his sword with his right hand and waved it in the faces of the reporters who quickly moved back a safe distance. The newspapermen became very quiet. Then the officer turned to face the back of the telegraph operator who was busy pounding the brass key. With his left hand the officer pulled his revolver from the holster and held the barrel to the back of the operator's head. The operator was slow to respond, so the officer cocked the hammer, with a click heard by all. At that exact instant, the telegraph operator stopped sending code, and without turning his head he asked for my message. I reached over his shoulder and handed him the piece of paper with the message. He quickly tapped out the message to the Medical Department in Washington asking for urgent medical supplies and assistance in the face of impending and cataclysmic battle.

The message sent, the staff officer turned and pointed the cocked pistol at the group of reporters and asked them if anyone had any complaints or comments. They had none. "General Meade does not tolerate any interference with the duties of his medical staff, particularly from reporters," he said, and then he uncocked his pistol and put away his side arms.

As I rode back to the hospital, I glanced back at the telegraph tent, and the operator was just sitting at the table waving off the reporters gathered around him. I suspect this story never made the *New York Herald*.

I returned to find the hospital in the same state as I left it. The surgery continued all morning on the six operating tables set up in the house. There were three tables in the dining room and three in another room. Two more operating tables were set up out in the front yard on bales of hay. The surgeons preferred working outside where light was better and ether could be safely utilized, since the chloroform supply was almost depleted. Ether could not be used inside around candles.

Surgeon Adams left the house to find our regiment in order to conduct the morning sick call. Assistant Surgeon St. James and I stayed in the field hospital to help the other surgeons try to get all of the wounded soldiers seen. St. James was extremely fatigued and could hardly grip the amputating knives. His right hand was swollen and stiff. He said, "Baldy, now is your chance to do some surgery. We'll see if Hoosiers can cut anything up except hog jowl." He would talk me through the procedures I had been so closely observing. I must admit his presence and direction gave me confidence. St. James was a conceited braggart, but he was also one of the best operating surgeons in the division.

The next wounded man in line to be treated was a young Rebel with a minié ball wound in his hip. As was the custom, I probed the wound with my index finger to try to locate the bullet. This young boy had a low pain tolerance and began to yell and thrash about. We couldn't restrain him well enough to complete the examination, so he was given precious chloroform, just enough so he was just barely put under. He continued squirming and moaning.

I couldn't feel the bullet with my finger. "I can feel that the greater trochanter of the femur is fractured, though," I told St. James. There were no loose bone fragments to remove. St. James told me to feel for the ball with a probe. "Your fingers are too short," he said. I introduced a long probe into the wound and could feel the bullet, which was just beyond the reach of my finger. The bullet forceps was positioned in the wound tract, but the bullet was hard to grasp.

St. James grabbed the ball with the forceps. "J_____ C_____, Baldy, I could teach an orangutan how to operate easier than you." Finally I was able to extract the bullet only as far as the entrance wound. I tugged on the forceps. "D— it, Baldy, incise the d— wound. Don't fiddle around all day pulling on that d— forceps." With these encouraging words I quickly incised the entrance wound with a scalpel while the patient was struggling on the table.

The flattened lead minié ball was then easily removed from the wound and clanked as I dropped it into a metal pan, and the young patient woke up to find me dressing his wound. I folded a piece of lint double and poured water on it; then placed it over the wound, securing it with a few strips of adhesive plaster. The recovering young Rebel was carried outside yelling and screaming, but otherwise in good condition.

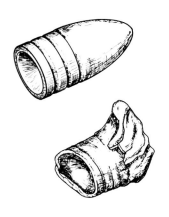

Spent Minié Ball

The next wounded man was a young, curly-headed lieutenant from the Third Corps whose foot was shattered by a shell fragment. He begged us to save his foot, but Teddy explained to him that the foot was damaged beyond repair and would have to come off. The chloroform supply was depleted. We decided to use ether after all, as there were no candles or other open flames in the room in the daytime and the windows were wide open for ventilation. The steward applied a tourniquet.

St. James, under terrific strain, had now cooled down a bit. "Now I'm going to talk you through a difficult amputation, and by G— I don't know why I'm doing it except my wrist is strained and I can't even lift a knife anymore. A Syme amputation removes the foot by disarticulation through the ankle joint, then a thin slice of the end of the tibia is sawed off with the malleolar projections so the heel pad can be placed over the end of the tibia. The os calcis must be carefully shelled out of the heel pad, and because of this the Syme amputation is one of the most difficult procedures we do."

He laughed his odd, high laugh, this time heavy with weariness. "And you, you, Hoosier boy, you are the one who has to save this boy's life. Get ready, Baldy."

I ignored the insults and nodded my readiness.

"Now if you can concentrate long enough, cut from here to here, and then from here to here," he pointed. "Cut! Cut, d— it. Hurry!" I worked as fast as I could. St. James was shouting at me with every step. Excising the heel bone from the heel pad was very difficult, especially with the dull knives. I was so weary I had to fight to stay awake. I recall really struggling. And then there was his harsh manner—it was all I could do to refrain from turning the knife on him.

But I finally completed the operation. The heel pad was sutured in place over the end of the tibia using silk thread, and adhesive strips were applied in the intervals between the sutures. The dressing consisted of pads of flannel and muslin secured with muslin roller bandages.

St. James offered what I supposed must be a compliment at the end of the case. "Doctor Baldwin, you're the slowest d— surgeon in this whole d— army. But your patient is still alive." Then he laughed again and turned his back to me and walked away.

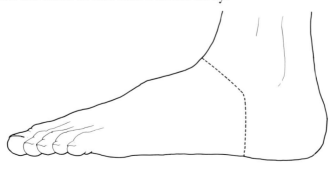

Incision for Syme Amputation

I almost seemed like a real surgeon after this case. I wiped the bloody knives off on my apron to clean them, and now I looked like a real surgeon. I held a knife in my teeth while helping to lift the patient off the table. Now I felt like a real surgeon.

The next patient brought to the table was an older soldier shot in the leg by a minié ball. The mid-portion of the tibia was shattered, and there was an exit wound in the calf. The man had lost a lot of blood and was pale with a rapid pulse. St. James quickly applied a tourniquet to prevent any more blood loss. If the man was to be able to wear an artificial leg, the circular technique of amputation would need to be done to conserve length below the knee. The flap technique would be faster to do, but it would sacrifice more length and make it difficult for this man to use an artificial leg.

I had seen enough amputations of the leg last night to feel confident enough to attempt this procedure. I made a circular incision through the skin around the leg. St. James assisted by retracting the skin with his good hand. I made another circular cut with the amputating knife through the muscle, and St. James retracted the muscle back from over the bone. A Catling knife was used to divide the muscle fibers in the interosseous space between the tibia and fibula; then I scraped the muscle from the tibia and fibula and used the capital saw to cut both bones. The fibula was cut a little shorter than the tibia, and the tibia was beveled on the front of the bone. The leg was removed and discarded, and I hooked the major arteries and veins with the tenaculum and ligated them with silk thread, the ends of which were brought out of the wound as a group. The tourniquet was released and the bleeding started immediately, but I controlled it by pressure on the wound, and wiped out the blood and clots with a sponge. The skin was pulled down over the bone ends and sutured loosely with silk thread using large curved needles. Adhesive straps were used between the sutures to assist in approximating the skin. The group of ligature thread coming out of one side of the wound was secured to the skin with a small strip of adhesive plaster. The shape of the amputation stump looked good, and when he had healed, this man would be able to walk with an artificial leg.

St. James complimented me again in his malignant way. "Not bad for a d—d Hoosier hick," he said.

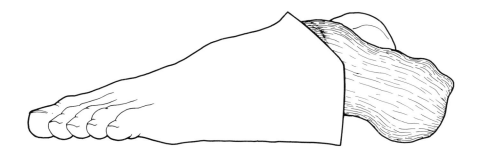

Specimen After Syme Amputation

The dressing was applied to the end of the stump, but was soon soaked with bright red blood. The man moaned as he woke up from the ether, and asked for water. He was very pale as he was carried out of the house. I wondered if he would survive his wound and my surgery. Perhaps I worried more than the other surgeons because I was new. St. James told me to get some coffee, so I got a tin cup full and went outside, where I threw myself down under a tree.

I wondered how much good we were really doing for these brave wounded soldiers. Those that survived their amputations still faced a lifetime with an amputation stump, possible chronic pain to their dying days, and who knew what mental distress from being limbless.

Where was Adams? I wondered if he had run into problems at sick call with the regiment, as I had not seen him for hours. Perhaps he was in the arms of Morpheus. Certainly all of us would envy him if he had been able to get a few winks of sleep.

I must have drifted off to sleep myself under that large oak for a few minutes or so, because I was awakened by the sound of exploding artillery shells. It was almost noon on that very long morning of July 3rd, and a few Rebel shells were coming over Little Round Top, our Weikert farmhouse being within range. The helpless wounded were in grave danger from the shell fragments and a few received new wounds, so quite reasonably, orders had been received while I was asleep to evacuate the farmhouse and move the hospital one mile southeast to some adjacent farms. Ayres' Division Field Hospital was to be set up on the Clapsaddle farm, and our (Barnes') Division Field Hospital was to go nearby to the Fiscel farm.

The ambulance train had been brought up in front of the house, and all were scurrying to evacuate the farmhouse and barn which were full of the wounded. Once the ambulances had finally cleared out, the supply wagons were brought up to take on the medical supplies and equipment. St. James rode his horse on to the Fiscel farm to meet the ambulances; all of the few remaining stewards and surgeons quickly packed up the medicine chests and amputation cases and loaded them on the wagons.

I personally supervised the loading of our regiment's amputation set and medicine chest onto the medical supply wagon for our brigade. I had been particularly diligent about packing the ether and chloroform, because none could be wasted, as the supply was dangerously low. Sporadic shells continued to land about the farmyard, terrorizing everyone, but miraculously no one was killed. There were, however, fragment wounds to a few of the medical detail and patients.

We saw the wagons on their way, and then we remaining surgeons, stewards, and attendants started walking southeast to the new field hospital locations. Chaplain O'Mara and I walked together. We wondered aloud how Surgeon Adams and Steward Franz had found the health of the regiment on sick call this morning. Certainly they had missed the scene of the most trying activity. We looked back over our shoulders once or twice, then left the farmyard to the shattering shells and the howling dogs of war. It was by now about mid-afternoon, and off in the distance we could hear the rumble of a massive Confederate cannonade of Cemetery Ridge, and the roar of Union artillery in response.

An area of farms became the Fifth Corps hospital cluster of division hospitals. When we arrived at the Fiscel farm, we were met with a line of ambulances waiting to be unloaded. The most seriously wounded soldiers were quickly carried into the small farmhouse and placed on the few beds and the small floor space available. We brought the rest of the wounded men into the large barn and placed them on what little hay was in the barn. Soon the buildings were full to capacity, so the rest of the patients were placed on the ground, with some of the lucky wounded having small shelter tents placed over them. The ambulances continued all afternoon and evening to disgorge patients from God knows where.

The chief surgeon for Barnes' Division assigned St. James and me as dressing surgeons, as several older surgeons had already been designated as the operating surgeons. Surgeon Adams had been among the earliest arrivals, and he had gone to work operating at once. St. James, as could have been predicted, was furious at being reassigned as a non-operating surgeon.

We started our rounds with the assistance of two musicians detailed as nurses to carry the dressing supplies and water. Our assignment was to treat the rows of patients on the bare ground, to replace lost dressings, and change only those dressings heavily soiled by mud or soaked by blood to conserve on the scant supply of bandages. Water was poured on dressings that had become dry. It was hard to make the men lying on the ground comfortable, because straw and blankets were also in short supply, but we did our best. Poor unfortunates!

Late in the afternoon a frantic courier from Fifth Corps headquarters rode up on a sweaty horse and shouted the exciting news that the center of the Union line had been attacked by a massive Confederate assault that made a breakthrough before finally being repulsed. The courier was already hoarse from repeatedly shouting the news as he rode by. "Huzzah! Huzzah! . . . Hancock's line held! The Rebs broke through, but our boys pushed them off the ridge, they did. Hancock's line held!" Soon he was gone.

We surgeons gathered in small groups; the wounded raised themselves on their elbows. Our Union line had held. The news was a great relief to the medical personnel and wounded soldiers alike, and all murmured or cried out their jubilation. We were not going to be defeated by Lee after all. Some even of the wounded shouted and jumped up and down for joy. "Hallelujah!" I said out loud in a hoarse voice.

I finally got a few hours of much needed sleep that night as I lay on the ground. I dreamt of home and Mary laughing and riding in a buggy with me on a sunny Sunday afternoon, bouncing till her hat jumped on her head. In this dream we went to beautiful White River and paddled a canoe downstream. But when we passed the bend near the Conner tract, in my troubled dream, it turned into the Niagara River, the falls near.

I was awakened by Chaplain O'Mara to come evaluate one of the mortally wounded soldiers lying off to the side of the hospital area. In the light of the lantern, I saw a pale, young private from the Fourth Michigan. He was not conscious, though his eyes were half open, and he was taking shallow gasps widely spaced in time. In a matter of only a few minutes he had taken his last breath of air. An orderly covered up the private's face with the blanket on which he lay.

I looked down the row of mortally wounded men, and at least a third already had their faces covered up by blankets or blue frock coats. I asked the orderly who these dying men were. They were mostly from the three brigades of Barnes' Division, but a few were from other divisions and corps. By dawn half of them would have their faces covered up. The burial detail would be busy in the morning.

The next day was the 4th of July, and when it rained heavily, I mused on how the heavens rained their displeasure so often after awful battles. The supply train with hospital supplies and tents finally arrived on the 5th. Seventeen hospital tents were pitched that day on the Fiscel Farm, but there were eight-hundred wounded men to shelter, including some Confederates. We continued our efforts. Tent flies and shelter tents were put up until all of the wounded finally had shelter.

It rained for three more days after that, and the wounded men lying on straw in the tents and the surgeons were all soaked. Sleeping on the wet ground on a wet blanket in wet clothes wrapped in a wet coat is miserable even when one is heavily fatigued. We had started with eleven surgeons, but eight became ill from nervous exhaustion. I was allowed to do more surgery; three surgeons including myself were able to operate while the other exhausted surgeons were recovering. However, it should be said that most of the surgery had actually been done by this time.

Chaplain by Dying Private

Surgeon Adams had worked two days and three nights without sleep. His last operation was an amputation of the leg of a Rebel on July 5th. The eye-strain and fatigue he endured were severe; indeed, he could hardly speak to St. James and me by the evening of July 5 and had to be helped to a rest area, where he collapsed. Because of severe exhaustion and an attack of blindness, he was honorably discharged from the army on July 7th, and he eventually returned home to Boston.

The night before Dr. Adams left, I had a word with him. He told me not to let St. James discourage me from mastering surgery. He said that the man was a surgeon highly trained far beyond others of his age, but that he was very critical of all doctors who were not as educated or naturally gifted as he was, which included most of the surgeons in the army. Adams conceded arrogant intellectualism was a failing of certain New England aristocrats, and he apologized for it on behalf of his fellow New Englanders. Certainly Adams was a kind and compassionate man, and he encouraged me to continue learning all that I could about surgery.

As if it were today, I can see him standing before me, his eyes under bandages to protect them from the light. "War is a great measuring rod. It severely takes our measure and tells us the type of men we are. You have performed well at your level of experience, and you have the makings of a surgeon," he said. He had always treated me fairly, and I hated to see him leave the army. We said goodbye, and that was the last time I ever cast eyes on Surgeon Adams. During this period he had sacrificed his career and even his health to fulfill the vows of his Hippocratic oath, and almost alone among the surgeons of the Northern Army, had gone to treat the men on the very field of battle. I have never seen his like again.

Shortly thereafter, Assistant Surgeon St. James got his promised promotion to Surgeon, replacing Adams as Surgeon of the Thirty-Second Massachusetts. Surgeon St. James, then, was with his regiment when the Army left Gettysburg to pursue Lee. As I was a U. S. Volunteer assistant surgeon and had been only temporarily assigned to the Thirty-Second, I was ordered to stay behind to help staff the division field hospital for Barnes' Division, where I was needed. Massachusetts would have to supply the assistant surgeon for the Thirty-Second to replace me.

Though very busy, I tried to write home whenever I had any spare minutes. Most of my letters were for Mary. I must admit the new lawyer in Noblesville was much on my mind. I also fretted about Father's ability to work the farm. Mother and Harriet must be doing menial labor this time of year, and I considered the harvesting of vegetables for the Indianapolis city market too heavy for women. I had heard very little from home; mail was irregular.

When the army moved south, the field hospitals were left very short-handed. The first round of surgery had been completed, and now of course there was much less surgery to do. Still, many Gettysburg patients remained under our care, and it was during this period that I encountered a man who was to become important to my service there.

My duties included changing dressings, treating fevers, and preparing the less severely injured soldiers for the trip to the railroad depot for the train ride to the general hospitals in the big eastern cities. Some Confederate prisoners were paroled to work as nurses and orderlies in our hospital on the Fiscel farm. Willard Newton was a sergeant in the First Texas Regiment of Robertson's Brigade in Hood's Division. Will was a good natured Texan whose kindness and sense of humor made him the most popular man in the hospital among the patients. He attended the wounded and sick as a nurse and returned when off duty to visit with the men and help them write letters home. I arranged for Will to assist me with my work, and we became comrades. He became my chief nurse, seeing that the dressings were kept wet with water and changed when badly soiled.

Nurse Newton was the first person to get some of our patients to laugh, and his good nature was the best medicine we had at the hospital. The wounded men loved to talk to Will; the ambulatory patients would gather around him in the evening to listen to his stories as well as find out what a real Rebel soldier was like.

I can see him yet in that Gettysburg darkness, speaking in hushed ghost-story tones to the men, who listened like children, ready to forget the hideous troubles of war listening to stories about Southern ha'nts.

One story I particularly recall was about a ghost in Will's home town in Texas. It seems that one of Travis' men got out of the Alamo one dark night late February in 1836 to get help for the Texans trapped in the Alamo. When the man left the Alamo, he was unarmed except for a knife given to him by James Bowie for protection. The man successfully got away and found help, but the relief column turned back and the man turned back with them. When the man later found out that all of the defenders in the Alamo had been killed by Santa Anna, he used Bowie's knife on himself. His ghost, said Will in his deep bass voice, had been seen on March 6th of every year since then just before sunrise running out of town in the direction of San Antonio. And Will had the man's knife to prove it, hidden in his blanket roll. He would make the patients promise to keep quiet if they wanted to see the knife, and show it to them as a reward for good behavior. I was told by a patient that it was the biggest and sharpest knife he had ever seen, and dried blood stains from the ghost were still visible on the big blade. Skeptically, I told the patient that I hoped to God that the stains were not Yankee blood.

During the second week of July the hospital was short on good food for nourishment for our recovering patients. One day a dirty young boy came wandering into the hospital area. We were busy, and the boy was shooed out of camp several times. Will befriended the lad, however, and learned that the boy's father had been killed at Chancellorsville in May, and that his mother made her home with her own mother on a farm just south of here.

I felt sorry for the poor youth but thought him a nuisance to the hospital. How wrong I was. The next morning a farm wagon pulled up to the hospital loaded with fresh bread, biscuits, pies, cakes, apple butter, and preserves. Sitting on the wagon was the dirty boy, but today washed and clean. Driving the wagon was a middle-aged Negro gentleman. An old lady known as Grandma Lizzie was sitting on the wagon along with her daughter, who was the dirty boy's mother.

The Negro driver was a former slave who had escaped by the underground railroad, coming up a little used route near here. He had almost been captured by his pursuers and had sustained many dog bites about his hands and forearms when he tried to fight off the pursuing hounds. Grandma Lizzie found him one day in a weakened condition on her farm and had him carried into her farmhouse, where she cared for him until he fully recovered. She officially bought his freedom and offered him a job, and now he was helping the old woman run her farm.

I was assisting with routine dressing changes when the farm wagon arrived, but I decided to take the time to greet the generous visitors.

Grandma Lizzie had come to help her wounded "boys." We escorted the ladies around the hospital while the wagon was unloaded at the cook tent. This food had arrived providentially, it seemed; the army and the Sanitary Commission had not yet furnished our hospital adequately because we were the furthest corps hospital from Gettysburg. The ladies remained all day, with Grandma Lizzie reading her Bible for some of the men in need of spiritual nourishment, and her daughter writing letters for those needing assistance in that vein.

Grandma Lizzie had brought a huge black pot of beans and corn bread. The dish became the instant favorite of the doctors, stewards, hospital attendants, and those patients without intestinal problems, and the Confederates especially appreciated Lizzie's cooking. The men begged her to return as often as she could so they might enjoy again the food sent from heaven. She promised she would return as long as she could be of some little help to her boys. The surgeons also acknowledged the great contributions she made to the hospital. Later, many a soldier testified that had it not been for Grandma Lizzie's beans and corn bread, they might well have not survived their wounds or the surgeons' knives. The word soon spread that the Fifth Corps Hospital was the best d— field hospital in Gettysburg, not because of the surgeons, but because we set a good table.

The next day being the Sabbath, Grandma Lizzie returned with a church choir. The choir walked among the hospital tents singing hymns. When they sang "The Solid Rock" there were few dry eyes. "On Christ, the sol-id Rock, I stand; all oth-er ground is sink-ing sand, All oth-er ground is sink-ing sand." "Amazing Grace" was also much appreciated and comforting to the men. " 'Tis grace hath brought me safe thus far." I believe we hit a turning point in the healing process of our hospital that Sunday with the church choir. After this visit the men seemed more determined not to give up their fight for life, nor did they believe the Union should, or would, give up the fight. Of a certainty, that dirty little urchin made a change in the corps hospital.

The Chief Surgeon of our division hospital had instructions from the Acting Surgeon-in-Chief of the cluster of hospitals of the Fifth Corps to transfer patients to the general hospitals back east as soon as they could be safely transported by rail. Each surgeon in our hospital had about the same number of patients. The more patients we moved out, the fewer patients we had left to treat. By late July most of the other surgeons had been transferred elsewhere, and it was rumored that all patients in and about Gettysburg would be consolidated into one large hospital. At that moment our hospital would be closed.

In the meantime, I needed to be tending the charges I had. Fevers resulting from suppurative wounds occupied my time in these hot and sultry days in late summer. I observed that all of the amputation stumps had become swollen, inflamed, and drained the expected "laudable pus."

But I was disappointed to find that many of the wounds broke open from the pressure of the swelling because the sutures pulled out through the skin flaps. I was further dismayed to find that some of the flaps retracted, exposing the end of the bone which was protruding through the wound.

The grisly sight of white bone protruding from an amputation stump not only horrified the nursing detail dressing the wound and the patient looking incredulously at his own truncated extremity, but the surgeons responsible for the man's care.

We observed that amputation wounds left open, allowing free drainage of pus, healed better than those wounds closed with sutures. The pus had to be allowed an easy way to get out of the body, it seemed. We removed sutures and evacuated pus in many of our amputation stumps. As the swelling of the wounds decreased, the drainage of pus also decreased and granulations formed in the wounds. Then adhesive strips could be applied to maintain better apposition of the flaps.

It was satisfying to observe progress. The surgeons who went south with their regiments missed the opportunity to know the results of their surgery, never realizing the problems we had caring for their patients, but they also never knew how we helped the healing.

One day Will took me to one of the hospital tents to look at the right leg wound of a corporal shot by a minié ball. The wound edges were black with liquefaction of the base and watery brown drainage. For the past few days the area of gangrene had enlarged, with a putrid odor emanating from the wound. The leg was swollen and red. This was the dreaded hospital gangrene, spreading toward the knee. Dressing changes daily had made no difference; the patient's condition was deteriorating. "He'll die, sure as you're born, if we don't do something," Will said and I agreed.

I thought that an amputation through the thigh could save this man's life. The Chief Surgeon, a Pennsylvania regimental surgeon from Harrisburg, examined the patient with me and agreed that amputation was the man's only hope to live. He suggested that I go ahead with the amputation as I thought best. I asked if he would stay and help me, but he had to leave for the rest of the day to attend a meeting to plan for establishing a general hospital east of town. Will set up the surgical table in front of the man's tent in the bright daylight, which was most satisfactory to me.

The corporal was placed on the table; the steward administered ether anesthesia. The amputation set was open on another table and the tourniquet placed high on the thigh and tightened. I planned to amputate the leg just above the knee. As I picked up the Catling knife, I realized that I was the only surgeon at the table, with only Will and one orderly to assist me. I had, of course, performed surgery with senior surgeons but now I was alone. I took a deep breath to calm my nerves.

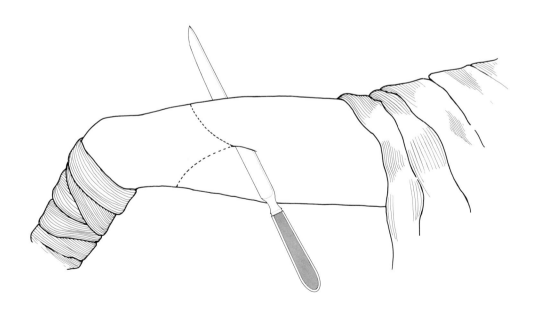

Amputation Through the Thigh

I carefully pushed the knife through the thigh to the femur. The knife was passed in front of the femur and out the other side of the thigh. The front flap was cut from inside out, and I executed the back flap in similar fashion. Will retracted the flaps, and the remaining muscle was scraped from the bone, the femur being divided with the capital bone saw. The leg was set onto a towel and carried away by an orderly, and the major vessels were ligated with silk thread. We released the tourniquet and controlled the usual bleeding with pressure. The skin flaps were loosely closed with silk sutures and adhesive straps on the skin, and dressings applied. The man soon awoke from the ether anesthesia; he had survived the operation. "Doctor? Doctor? . . . Am I going to make it?" he asked.

"Corporal, you have a strong constitution. The surgery went well," I replied.

"Oh—Thank you Doctor." He smiled wanly. "You're a fine surgeon."

Will patted me on the back. And since Will would be taking care of this man, I knew the patient would be in good hands. I was a happy man.

On another occasion, a patient with a draining thigh wound became very ill. Will reported to me that the man was having trouble swallowing liquids, and he had become restless and irritable. I went to examine the man, and found he had a fever and was having spasms and stiffness of the jaw. In fact he had a fixed, sardonic smile from spasms of his facial muscles—lockjaw. The man had tetanus and would probably die; treatment in such cases was hopeless. I could amputate the extremity through the thigh high above the wound. However, the mortality rate of amputation through the upper thigh was high, and with tetanus, it would be certain death. The chief surgeon was summoned for his opinion. He took one look at the poor fellow and said it was hopeless, then he left. He was right, as the poor man died the next morning. We saw more than one case of lockjaw, and all died.

A Mrs. Gatewood came to the hospital to see her wounded son. He had just died the day before and was buried in a shallow grave near the hospital. She was brought to me, since I had taken care of her son. I had to break the bad news to her as she thought him alive. This was a difficult situation, for she cried and screamed loudly, attracting a crowd of attendants and patients. "You killed my son! You murderers! You murdered my son! I begged him not to volunteer. This awful war against the Constitution is to blame . . . Devil take Lincoln! D— the Union!" she cried with a vengeance as Will and I took her to my tent to talk to her. Soon Chaplain O'Mara arrived to comfort her. I was really glad to still have O'Mara around. He was supposed to be with the brigade in Virginia and was probably considered a deserter by now.

After Mrs. Gatewood had calmed herself, Will escorted her to the grave which was marked with a wooden headboard. A traveling embalmer had set up shop in camp, and he came creeping up to help her with the body. Will instructed the burial detail to dig up the remains; then the poor lady identified the bloated body of the emaciated young man in the muddy army blanket as her son. The members of the detail carefully wrapped the body in a new army blanket and transported it by wagon to the embalmer's tent. I must say the man's tasks were executed quietly and efficiently, and finally the embalmed body was placed in the wooden box and loaded on a wagon for the trip to the railroad depot. The lonely mother expressed her thanks for all we had done for her son, and then she was helped onto the wagon for the ride to meet the train that would take her and her only son home.

The mail was delivered to the hospital one day, and I received a number of letters during this time. There were two letters from Mother. She wrote that Father's rheumatism of neck and back was much better, and he was able to work some in the fields. The men in his church had helped out almost daily while he was down, and the corn was over waist high. I was heartened by this wonderful news.

The other letter was from my dear one. She acknowledged getting three of my many letters written since the battle, but her letter was short and rather cold, I thought. The young lawyer had asked her hand in marriage. She told him no, that she would wait for me to return to be fair to me. She did tell me about the palatial new house that was being started across the street from the county courthouse. Also, she mentioned that they went for a ride with box lunches in his buggy every Sunday to the White River. I became unusually angry after reading this letter. Who was this shirker who had usurped my place while I served our country?

Several days each week it was my duty to attend to the patients transported to the railroad depot for transfer to the large general hospitals in the East. The ambulances routinely picked up the wounded men early in the morning and headed north up the Taneytown Road, a trip that was usually uneventful, except for the passage through town when the civilians would stop to watch the ambulances slowly lumber by. Some of the less severely wounded men would wave energetically to the onlookers, who would initiate sporadic cheers for the men. The children would run alongside the ambulances, because the men would shout out Union slogans and talk to them. Sometimes this would get the adults excited, and cheers and words of encouragement would pass between the wounded soldiers and civilian spectators. All in all these occasions were felicitous, because the wounded men were taking another step toward home.

One such trip to the railroad depot turned into a disaster. The ambulances were passing through town on what seemed to be a routine run, with the wounded soldiers and civilian onlookers cheering each other as usual. The ambulance train stopped while a stretcher-bearer ran back to my ambulance with the news that one of the patients in the second ambulance was hemorrhaging severely from his thigh wound. I could hear shrieks from the front of the train as I ran to the back of that ambulance and leaped on board.

I instantly recognized him as one of my patients by the name of Benjamin. His last name eludes me at this distance in time. An attendant had the presence of mind to hold a dressing firmly on the wound. Bright red blood soaked the dressing and ran down the thigh forming a pool of blood on the floor of the ambulance. Pressure slowed the bleeding but did not stop it. The man was pale, but he had been pale since the minié ball had pierced his thigh. This individual had been under my care since the corps hospital had been set up at the Fiscel Farm, and I had written his family telling them he was doing well and would soon be sent to a general hospital in Washington. I realized the femoral artery wall must have necrosed and blown during the bumpy ride into town.

I ordered the ambulance to cut out of line and turn right at the next corner, as the streets were too narrow to turn around. The ambulance driver raced us back to the field hospital while we tried to stop the arterial bleeding by pressure , an exercise in futility. The poor screaming wretch suffered with each bump, and the ambulance seemed to be in the air at times, with the civilians on the streets appearing puzzled as we streaked by creating a great deal of commotion. Buggies and wagons rapidly pulled to the side of the street to let us pass, with our driver cursing at them at the top of his lungs; certainly the good people of Gettysburg heard some new oaths that morning. Sad to say, the pale man's pulse rate was becoming more rapid and feeble. A tourniquet had to be used high on the thigh to finally stop the profuse bleeding as we raced on toward the hospital.

The ambulance halted in front of the hospital. The patient was moved by stretcher and placed screaming onto the operating table. Several surgeons arrived in timely manner to administer some chloroform to calm the man down so we could stop his hemorrhage. The tourniquet was released, triggering bright red arterial bleeding from deep within the thigh wound. We packed the wound with astringents and dressings, but the bleeding could not be stopped. The doomed man was bleeding to death from a secondary hemorrhage, which we always feared with deep wounds around the major arteries.

I finally decided upon surgery, and the tourniquet was reapplied, as I quickly incised the wound to expose the femoral artery. The side of the artery had necrosed and blown out. The wound involved the proximal portion of the thigh, and I would not be able to ligate the artery from another incision higher up the thigh. There was no choice but to ligate the artery just proximal to the damaged segment. The femoral artery was quickly exposed, and I passed the aneurism needle around the artery. A silk ligature was passed around the vessel and securely tied. As the tourniquet was released, there was back-bleeding from the injured artery. I placed a second ligature distal to the damaged vessel. Now the hemorrhage was slowed down to a degree I could control with pressure dressings and astringents.

The man was as white as a ghost when he recovered from the anesthetic. His pulse was rapid and thready, but I was satisfied that at least he was alive. This had become a very harrowing morning for one that had started out as a leisurely trip to the train station. The patient must have been very disappointed that his trip home had been so unexpectedly interrupted. I just hoped that he might survive this terrible complication.

Later that day, Benjamin's leg continued to be cold and without pulses. The collateral circulation was insufficient to keep his leg alive. The foot and leg would develop the expected gangrene and amputation through the thigh would be needed. Unfortunately, the poor soul was in dreadful condition, as he had bled down too far to recover, and he soon died.

In spite of all the death I had seen and the calluses that had developed over my sensibilities, I was deeply distressed. What would his family think? I had written to say he was getting well. All of the death, pain, misery, and bad luck was taking its toll on me. Chaplain O'Mara saw my plight, and he sat me down for a long discussion in my tent. He listened a lot. We talked about the war, President Lincoln, and the South, death, and the purpose of life. We spoke about God, and although I had the blue-blacks, I began to regain my composure. We prayed. My pessimism lessened. I sat down to write a personal letter to the parents of the deceased, and having O'Mara there for support was a big comfort. As Chaplain O'Mara departed, he told me he would head south in the morning to join the gallant men of the Thirty-Second Massachusetts and the rest of the brigade. We said goodbye, and after he was out of sight, I wondered where I might be sent when our hospital closed.

The Fifth Corps Hospital was open until August 2nd, when it was closed. All remaining patients were transferred to Camp Letterman, and I went with them.

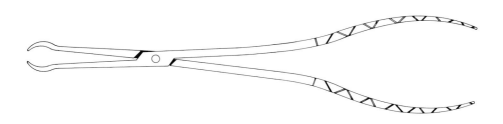

Bullet Forceps

Chapter VIII.

Camp Letterman General Hospital

August 2, 1863

I rode in the last ambulance to leave the Fiscel farm for Camp Letterman. The line of ambulances wound its way north up Baltimore Street through Gettysburg to the square. The ambulances then turned east on York Street to York Pike and then northeast for almost a mile to the General Hospital. The Hanover, Hanover Junction and Gettysburg Railroad tracks ran parallel just north of York Pike, as I recall. A hospital train carrying the wounded from the railroad depot was picking up speed as it passed our ambulances on the Pike. The engineer and fireman waved as the steam engine passed us and saluted with a blast on the whistle. Soldiers on the last car gave a cheer of encouragement to us as the steam train pulled away into the distance and soon disappeared, leaving only a plume of dissipating smoke and the receding sound of the steam whistle.

The hospital was a sight to behold. There were hundreds of large hospital tents set up in neat rows, covering a large area. We were directed to the tents waiting in preparation for our patients. Soon the ambulances were unloaded and left to pick up other loads of wounded from the remaining field hospitals in and around Gettysburg.

I had been officially reassigned to Camp Letterman, so I reported to the hospital director for further orders. This gentleman, whose name eludes me, informed me that I was to be assigned as a ward surgeon treating sixty patients housed in eight tents. A wagon brought over the baggage from the Fifth Corps Hospital and unloaded it at the entrance to Camp Letterman on the south side of York Pike. Loaded down with all of my remaining few possessions, I moved among the hospital tents and located my quarters, which were to be shared with another surgeon.

I discovered my new tentmate was Assistant Surgeon Sterling Maxwell from New York City. Our patients were in adjacent areas, and we were to work together when surgery was necessary. I was delighted to find that Doctor Maxwell was a most kind and Christian human being, quite a contrast from Doctor St. James of Boston. We would get along famously, I decided. In passing I wondered what had happened to St. James, as I had heard nothing from him, nor did I ever expect to hear.

Doctor Maxwell gave me a quick tour of the hospital grounds. South of the main area of hospital tents was a smaller area of hospital shelters for the wounded officers. Just south of this was the deadhouse and the graveyard, a macabre trail of progression which many unfortunates had already made. An embalming tent was nearby for those dead whose relatives wanted to have the fallen dear one's body sent home for a proper burial.

On the north end of the camp was the cookhouse. Looking west, one could see the churches and houses of Gettysburg off in the distance, while if one turned his gaze to the east, he could see a pleasant area of forests.

Across York Pike to the north were the tents for the Sanitary Commission and beyond that, the railroad tracks. The hospital train was to stop across from the camp, and the patients would be carried on litters across the pike to be loaded onto the hospital cars. Once the train was loaded, the steam engine would slowly pull away from Camp Letterman with its cars full of happy convalescing soldiers headed for the large general hospitals in the Eastern cities such as Washington, Baltimore, and Philadelphia.

The tour over, I headed to my assigned hospital tents to make morning visits with my new patients. Five of my tents contained Union wounded. Two of my tents had Confederate wounded, and one tent had half Union and half Confederate wounded. I met the steward, a man whom I had worked with before, who had his notebook and pencil ready to take my orders, and we started our visit in the first tent. Each tent had a soldier detailed to be a nurse assigned to it. The two Confederate tents had Confederate nurses, but the mixed tent had a Union soldier as nurse.

As the nurse told me what he knew about the wounded man, I examined each patient. I noted that the ticket hanging at the foot of each wooden folding cot was almost blank except for the patient's name and rank. None of the tickets had been filled out for company, regiment, disease or injury, or date of admission. These rounds were time-consuming, as I removed the dressings to examine each wound. The first tent took me over an hour just to see the eight patients.

Unfortunately, the acute shortage of doctors had left these nurses unsupervised, and the results were truly dismal. All of the dressings were dry, soiled, and odorous. I removed each dressing and found a pool of thick yellow, brown, or green pus. Nearly every wound had maggots squirming around. A few wounds contained so many maggots that they fell out of the wound, wiggling onto the bedding.

Before I knew what was occurring, the steward came forward and with great alacrity poured a little chloroform on the wounds of a couple of the sufferers, thus causing them to cry out in pain.

"That'll take care of the maggot problem," he muttered. It did not seem to me to be a very good treatment. He left in answer to a call from another tent.

"How often do you change these dressings?" I asked of the private detailed as a nurse. "I'm not sure, Sir. No one's instructed me yet on what to do," the private replied honestly. "I do pour water on the dressings each morning to moisten them," he went on. "And if a dressing comes off, I put on another." The patients had just arrived here a few days ago, and most still had the original dressings with which they arrived. The inexperienced private had only been assigned as a nurse that week and was apparently expected to learn on his own

This nurse, whose name was Private Zimmerman, described his duties, largely self-imposed. He would attempt to feed the men three meals a day. Some could only sip soup, and these had to be spoon-fed, a time-consuming task. The rest could feed themselves, but needed some help. Helping the men with voiding was a problem, because the urine had to be carried out of camp for disposal in a large trench sink, a lengthy, tiresome task. Taking care of the stool was a worse problem, especially when the men had diarrhea, which was frequent. Bed pans had to be carried out of camp to dump into the sinks.

Bathing the men was also quite difficult. All of the water for personal cleansing had to be carried in buckets by hand, and none of the men in his tent was ambulatory. They were all severely injured; if they weren't, they would have been evacuated by now. "Private, your patients are receiving wretched care!" I found myself yelling at the poor man, but as I spoke I realized that he was doing the best job that he could with what little he knew about medical care. In a way, we all were.

I was aware that I would need more help to properly care for these wounded men, and my thoughts turned inevitably to Willard Newton, who had been paroled and was planning to return home to Texas. I had actually caught a glimpse of him this morning when he was helping to strike the hospital tents and load them on the supply wagons, but we had not communicated in quite a while. I formed the resolution to locate Will quickly before he left Gettysburg.

I borrowed a horse and rode quickly over to the Fiscel farm. My heart sank—the farm was completely deserted—and what a state it was in. I suppose I had not noticed it when we were in the midst of all of our busy days, but it was as if a ghoulish reaper had come down with the specific purpose of destroying it as a farm. The rail fences had all been used up as firewood, and the grass and crops had been stomped down to the bare dirt. Wagon and ambulance wheel ruts were all over the fields, refuse in heaps.

A Grim Reaper, truly, is war, and it would be many a day before this farm knew the blissful routine of rural life.

Will was gone, and I wondered which way he had gone. He would head south, I supposed. I rode over to the Taneytown Road and turned south. A few miles south I saw a lone figure trudging along with a blanket roll slung across his shoulder. On catching up with the paroled Rebel, I saw it was Will.

"Will, stop a moment! I need your help. Come to Camp Letterman with me."

He stared up at me wide-eyed. "Hello Doc. I didn't expect to see you no more."

"Will, you have got to come with me to Camp Letterman. There is so much to do. I need you."

He thanked me kindly but refused. It was time for him to go home. He was paroled, he had worked a whole month for the Yankees, it was more'n they deserved. His family needed him more'n we did. Or so he asserted.

I got off my horse. "Will, listen to me," I said, in my desperation. "I beg you to come to Camp Letterman. I have sixty badly wounded men to care for, and there are only eight nurses to help me. I can't do it without more help."

"Sorry Doc," he told me. "It ain't my problem no more. Wish you luck, Doc. You're a good man. Now move your Yankee horse."

I refused to move. I told him that twenty of my patients were Confederates, sick, his own people. "Wouldn't they stay for you? What kind of people are you Southerners? Don't you know the meaning of the word honor?" This I demanded to know.

He stared at me, angrily. "Listen Doc. If I had a gun I might shoot you on the spot. Then again, I might not. You know you're my friend. Yes, those men might stay for me. And I might stay for them . . .. D— you Yankees. I'll come with you."

We rode double back to Gettysburg, a Yankee surgeon and a Rebel soldier, generating some stares from citizen and soldier alike. The hospital director ignored the fact that I had recruited a paroled Rebel to help as a nurse, as there were a number of Confederate nurses already in camp helping with the care of the Confederate wounded. I gave Will a Union uniform to wear while he was on duty with me, and later I was fortunate enough to arrange for Will to receive the same pay as the other men of the hospital corps, a most generous $20.50 a month. I also secured for him some civilian clothes to wear when he was off duty so he could move about in town without any provoking encounters.

I resumed rounds late that afternoon starting over with the first tent. The nurse I had spoken to was conscientiously at work, following my instructions to change all of the dressings daily and to keep them wet with water. The steward, Will, and I moved on to the second tent. Each tent was the same awful situation I had encountered before. The nurses were untrained. The dressings were rotten. The miserable wounded soldiers were desperately ill and long-suffering. Most were malnourished, pale, gaunt, and sad. We were all in for a lot of work. I would have to get more help.

After working our way through the five tents with Union wounded, we arrived at the tent with four of our own men and four Confederates, a

Mason-Dixon tent, if you will. These patients were convalescing nicely for some reason, and some were up with crutches or able to sit on the side of the bed. Things were looking better, here, where North and South met. Could it have been because of the interest generated by having "the enemy" close at hand, having to be lived with?

The last two of my eight tents contained Confederates only. Will brightened up on seeing so many fellow Rebels. But on closer inspection, it became evident that most of these Rebel wounded were severely ill, and some of them would probably never see home again. One such young Rebel had a high fever and was hallucinating. In delirious shrieks he would call out for his mother. After a moment of silence he would tell her how much he enjoyed seeing her face again. More silence was followed by more shrieks for "Mama."

I assigned Will the job of overseeing the care of the Confederate patients, and the nurses in these tents were given instructions that Nurse Newton was the nursing supervisor and that they were expected to take orders from him. Will had become so knowledgeable in military medicine at the corps hospital that the nurses in my section looked up to him to teach them their job without difficulties.

In the next few days, conditions improved greatly. The patients were cleaner, ate better, and some of them even smiled a time or two. However, two Confederate patients died during this time. This caused a slight problem. In the Mason-Dixon tent an argument broke out over medical care. The Rebels complained that the Yankee patients got better care than they did, with the Yankee patients escalating the argument by suggesting that the Rebels had no rights for any medical attention, not even poor care. Yelling started up among the two sides, and soon the patients were throwing bed pans and cups at each other.

Then a Union amputee with his left leg missing above the knee got up on his crutches to attack a Confederate patient sitting on the edge of his cot. The Confederate stood up on wobbly legs, but he was an upper extremity amputee with both hands missing at the wrists. As the Yankee amputee reached the bedside of the standing Rebel, the Rebel kicked the left crutch spilling the Yank across the cot. The Yankee struck the poor man across the ends of his upheld forearm stumps with his crutch.

The Rebel let out a loud Rebel yell and kicked the Yankee on the end of his left thigh amputation stump. Then the Yankee, writhing in pain, let out a loud Union yell and tripped the attacking Rebel. This Rebel shouted out in pain, and by this time everyone in the tent was yelling.

The medical staff and nurses came running from all directions and entered the tent. Although there was a lot of screaming going on, none of the patients in the tent was standing. It was difficult at first for the nursing staff to determine what had happened. No one was fighting or able to fight when the steward, Will, and I arrived and began trying to put things to right.

The two sides didn't want to discuss it with me, so I told Will to address problems in this tent. Will spent a long time in private talking to these men. I cannot say precisely what he told them, but that was the last I heard of that argument. Will apparently punished these tent warriors by keeping them all in the same tent. I had wanted them separated, but Will's was the better plan.

Oddly enough, eventually this became my best tent. Those that had hands helped those that didn't. Those with legs did the walking for those without legs. These men helped each other after that like brothers. Word came to me that Nurse Will told them that if they wanted the best care, they had to pitch in and help each other for a change. Otherwise, they would get nothing special. That must have done it, because this was the model tent for my section.

I easily got to know Doctor Maxwell. He was not only a friendly person, but he was a natural teacher who taught me a lot about the diagnosis and treatment of various diseases one encounters in military service. In an atypical way, he was more interested in treating diseases, and less interested in treating fractures or doing surgery. I consulted with him daily, and he was glad to see certain difficult cases with me; in fact, we traded patients from time to time. I transferred a severe case of diarrhea to him, and he wanted me to take over the case of a badly fractured ankle.

When his patient with the severe ankle fracture arrived in one of my tents, I was caught off guard when the patient called out to me, "Doctor Baldwin, it's me. You waited for me, didn't ya? I knowed you would, 'cause we're from the Thirty-Second, ain't we?" I instantly recognized

Corporal Jacob Phillips, and recalled that he had been rescued from a hungry herd of swine in the woods near the wheatfield. He had sustained a badly displaced compound fracture of the ankle with fracture of the lower end of the fibula and dislocation of the lower end of the tibia inwards. His had been a fracture of the internal malleolus of the tibia with the end of the tibia sticking out of the skin and the foot displaced to the outer side of the ankle and rotated outward. I had wondered why he did not ever arrive at the Weikert farmhouse on the morning he was found near the wheatfield.

Corporal Phillips informed me that he had been placed in an ambulance with wounded soldiers from Caldwell's Division of the Second Corps, and so was taken to a Second Corps field hospital at a white frame farmhouse near Cemetery Ridge. That night he was placed on a blanket in the front yard of the house next to a Confederate general from Mississippi. The general, whose name, I am quite sure, began with a "B," had been shot through the chest and was having great problems breathing. He had also been shot twice in the leg. The Rebel general was a large man, and he cursed the Yankees and begged for water much of the night. Phillips finally fell asleep, and on awaking after sunrise, found the general was gone.

Phillips was then transferred to the Second Corps Hospital for treatment of his compound ankle fracture. Dressing surgeons placed a bandage over the wound at the inner side of his ankle. Then a wooden Dupuytren's splint was applied to the inner side of his leg over a large pad and secured with roller bandages about the foot and near the knee to hold his ankle in better alignment.

I examined Corporal Phillips. His foot was still somewhat deviated and rotated outward, and even if it healed like this, I doubted if he would ever be able to walk on it very well. I removed the splint and dressings, and found that the wound was draining laudable pus and had redness and swelling about the wound. There was evidence of some healing of the wound, but the fracture still had a jog of painful movement. An amputation through the leg seemed like good treatment, and I suggested this to Jacob. He explained that the other surgeons had also wanted to amputate, but he had refused their recommendations time and time again.

"Doc, I want you to save my foot." I assured him I would try, and so the wound was dressed, the ankle fracture was realigned as best I could do it, and the Dupuytren's splint was reapplied and secured to the limb.

He was issued crutches so he could be up and about. The outlook was not good in my opinion. "Doc, I still dream of medical school," he called out to me as I walked from the tent. Oh, how I hoped he would be able to do that some day. He was such a nice young fellow. I stopped and turned toward the tent to say something. "Doc, do you reckon they allow cripples in medical school?" he called out from the tent.

After a pause, I replied something like, "Corporal Phillips, they would be honored to have you in their medical school. A lot of America is going to have to allow cripples in every part of its life." And well they should. The flower of the nation's manhood now walked on one leg or threw with one hand, the other having been given to pay honor's debt.

I approached Doctor Maxwell about the need for more assistance with nursing care. He informed me that we would have trained ward masters arriving any day now, which might ameliorate our difficulties. He then suggested that we visit the superintendent of the Sanitary Commission that day. We walked across the pike to the Sanitary Commission tents. The superintendent was a prominent minister and proved very helpful to us, saying yes, they could provide experienced volunteer civilian nurses to help out with nursing care. He would bring two nurses over to our wards in the morning.

Later that day, I had the good fortune to receive a letter from Steward Franz with the Thirty-Second Massachusetts Regiment in Virginia. Surgeon St. James, he allowed, was more conceited than ever, and now he was demeaning his new assistant surgeon, who was also from Boston. Our comrades were in good spirits, but the regiment was a much smaller one, of course, since Gettysburg. Ludwig Franz wrote that he and the men missed me. I missed them too, and I wished them well. I sat down to write and tell them so.

The next morning, the Sanitary Commission superintendent drove up in his buggy with the volunteer nurses he had promised. I stared at them as they stepped down. They were two young ladies. Miss Ruth Davenport was a volunteer nurse from Massachusetts, and she could work in my ward of eight tents. The other nurse would be assigned to Doctor Maxwell's ward. The Reverend would bring the nurses to the wards each morning and pick them up each evening. I inquired of myself as to how I felt about female nurses and decided I would let circumstances prove the merit of the situation. Besides, we needed every human hand we could get.

Miss Davenport was in her mid-twenties. She had light brown hair in a bun, dark eyes, and fine features. She was pleasant and very attractive, and personal aspects began to enter our professional relationship almost at once. Sweet scent, the starchy look of a woman's shirtwaist, the delicate look of white hands were now a part of the hospital day. I found myself wondering if somehow, like Aladdin, I had been transported to the city of paradise. She had appeared out of noplace in this tent city of misery. I hoped that we might have a chance to get acquainted in the next few weeks.

I soon saw she hardly seemed to notice me, being all business, going to work immediately. Nurse Davenport, as a matter of fact, considered herself an expert in nursing care. She issued commands to the male nurses as if she were a major. She was highly critical of the care given to the patients and argued daily with Will about nursing matters. She also was critical of my management of the patients and disputed with me in front of the attendants and patients. "The beds are filthy and the sheets look like they have never been cleaned. And the patients are filthy, too. They must be bathed daily. The tents must be swept out twice a day, and the patients must be moved out into the sunlight every day. And the food isn't even fit to give to a pet dalmatian." It would be hard to get to know this young lady; certainly I wasn't sure where she fit into the hospital chain of command.

Truly I thought Maxwell had gotten us into a hoopoe's nest. This female nurse was set to disrupt our routine and upset all of the male nurses as well as the patients. On the other hand, she had received a few months of training in New York City before working for several months in various general hospitals in Philadelphia and Baltimore. Patients did seem to be improving under her regime. Perhaps these persnickety ways had merit. I determined to continue to give her a fair chance to prove women could help take care of wounded men as well as their own sex.

We had, of course, some respite from the routine—Doctor Maxwell invited me to join him and some of the other surgeons on a trip into town with some of the volunteer civilian lady nurses. I was reluctant, given the acrimony in the tents, but agreed to go. We picked up the nurses and drove into Gettysburg, an unauthorized use of an ambulance, which Maxwell thought that we should venture anyway. The little group of doctors and nurses spent the evening in a basement tavern for supper. The tavern was built over a spring which was used to cool the milk, beer, and wine, and the dark room was lit by flickering candles. The nurses looked especially attractive in the flickering light, particularly Miss Davenport. Our group, enjoying the welcome break from the gloom of our daily work, soon became very jovial. The ladies abstained from the spirituous liquors, but the surgeons sampled some of the wine and beer.

This was my first chance to converse with Miss Davenport without disputations over patient care. She indicated to me she was from a well-to-do family in Cambridge. I asked friendly, leading questions. Then I received startling news. She asked if I knew Doctor Theodore St. James. I managed to say that I had been in his regiment, the Thirty-Second Massachusetts Regiment. She was very proud of the fact that he was now Surgeon of the Thirty-Second. In a dismaying coincidence I was disappointed to learn that Ruth considered herself his fiancee. No wonder she had given me such a difficult time at the hospital; she was, unconsciously, taking up where St. James had left off. Anyone who loved him would have to be the mother of all shrews.

We rode the ambulance back to the camp, returning "in spirits" that night—at least the men were. I was feeling about two sheets to the wind from the alcohol when Will met me at my tent with some bad news. Another Confederate soldier had died. Because most of my deaths had been Confederates, I felt embarrassed, but it seemed that the hand I was dealt was stacked against me, for the Rebel wounded were sicker than my Union wounded.

We discussed the Confederate dead problem that night. I decided to have Will and Nurse Davenport concentrate their energies on the remaining Confederate soldiers. Confederate deaths put us in a dishonorable light, to say nothing of the humanitarian considerations. The challenge of keeping his fellow Rebels alive was one that Will was happy to accept.

As we closely watched the Southern contingent, we realized it was necessary to do an amputation below the knee for a Confederate soldier with a leg that had developed hospital gangrene around the ankle wound. We had, of course, tried to salvage the leg. The amputation was done in the morning in the sunlight on a table in front of my row of tents. Doctor Maxwell assisted me and supervised the steward giving the ether anesthesia.

Oddly, Will and Nurse Davenport insisted on washing the leg with soap and water prior to making the incision. I acquiesced, because I had learned not to argue with those two. Will and Ruth were also washing my amputation instruments with soap and rinsing them with hot water. "Some in Boston believe the contagious diseases are caused by harmful matter which is in secretions," Nurse Davenport said. Pshaw, I thought in my ignorance, the hot water will only make the instruments rust faster. The amputation procedure went well as a group of medical staff looked on. As most of the patients were convalescing, not much surgery remained to be done, so operative procedures attracted an audience.

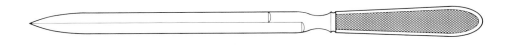

Catling (Catlin) Knife

A strange thing happened to this patient. The usual surgical wound healed, of course, with copious drainage of "laudable pus," necessary, as we then thought, for proper healing of the wound.

But this patient healed differently. The amputation stump drained some bloody drainage for a few days, and then it dried up. The stump healed faster, and without the usual "laudable pus." Doctor Maxwell said he had seen this healing manifestation once or twice before, but he did not know why that phenomenon occurred. This was not the way wounds were supposed to heal. The patient was comfortable and happy. Could the odd theory about contagious matter be true? Had they washed it off?

Of course we in the medical profession discovered later that that was, indeed, the case. How many we could have saved had we known that fact universally then.

The next few weeks passed quickly. Miss Davenport became a little more cordial to me, but yet she seemed committed to criticizing me in front of the attendants and patients. I was, she contended, trying to restrict the patients with fevers, and they needed more liquids. I countered that pushing water down them kept the attendants busy emptying the urinals; this sort of treatment embarrassed me almost daily, but she was an independent woman and was not under the control of the army. Sometimes I wished to have her under my control, she an enlisted man and I an officer. Insubordination would not then have been allowed!

But all things considered, my patients were getting healthier and stronger, thriving on good care and better food. Some of them were up with crutches, and no one had died over the past few weeks. My ward was a model of modern military medicine thanks to my dedicated nurses, especially Will and Miss Davenport. Some of my nurses were transferred to other wards to be instructors in nursing care. I had fewer patients each week, as they were gradually evacuated by train to the big general hospitals in the East. Camp life was finally getting down to a calm routine, and I had more time for recreation.

In a strange way, and perhaps because of necessity and the odd circumstances of proximity, Miss Davenport and I found ourselves drawn together after hospital hours, taking frequent walks in the evenings around the camp grounds and occasionally going into town for dinner and wine.

Perhaps it was because I had determined to thrust Mary from my mind. No letter had come; she and her lawyer friend were probably preparing to walk beneath the bridal rose arch. I might have been falling in love with Miss Davenport, but her conversation was still filled with reminiscences of St. James which made me uncomfortable. I certainly enjoyed her good looks and the charming companionship of a lady.

Mail call was more reliable now. News from the family was generally encouraging—Father was able to keep up with the farm work since he had frequent help from the men in his church. His rheumatism had steadily improved. Finally a letter came from Mary in which she wrote that her lawyer friend was putting pressure on her to marry him this winter when his new house would be ready. She had not said yes, but in fact, they had been looking at furniture together for his house, an occupation she seemed to find particularly agreeable. My helplessness angered and saddened me; Mary's affections for me had gradually grown dimmer in my absence, and what could I do about it, far away out here as I was? And, I thought, anyway, who was I? What did I have to offer her? Nothing. I was a man who was rapidly growing older and without prospects. Various paths had closed in my life, failure had become all too well known. I had come to this war to become a regimental surgeon, and I had not even been able to do this. I had best forget Mary.

One day I heard there was to be an appreciation ball at the Pennsylvania College in the College edifice building for the medical personnel taking care of the wounded. This was to include the medical staff officers, stewards, and ward masters as well as the volunteer nurses, members of the Sanitary Commission, and certain invited guests from the community. I wished to escort Miss Davenport to the collation, because, as I have said, I sensed an improvement in our friendship recently. Apparently I asked too late. She had accepted the invitation of a surgeon with the rank of major.

There would not really be enough young ladies to go around, so I decided not to attend. The afternoon of the ball, however, I received a note from the lucky major, who needed a favor. It seems he had come down with a severe case of the quickstep and would be unable to accompany Miss Davenport to the dance. He needed someone to stand in his stead. I sent him a note: I would be honored to come to his assistance.

The ball was a gala affair. Ruth was attired in an elegant mauve evening gown, one of the new hoop-less skirts, and was certainly the most attractive young lady there. I felt fortunate to have the honor of her company. My fellow officers treated me with good-natured envy. The ball began nicely with the grand march from Chopin, with a great brigade brass band wearing their dress uniforms.

The full, rich sound of the brass instruments vibrated through the ballroom with the scintillating cadences of marches and quicksteps. Popular favorites during the evening as I recall, for me were the "Palmyra Schottische" and "La Marseillaise." The evening was a truly memorable one. I filled the cards of several belles and we waltzed, polka-ed and executed the figures of the schottische, quadrille, galop, and reel, all on my part clumsily, I am sure.

Miss Davenport danced with many other officers at the ball; her card was, of course, full early in the evening. The Eastern officers proved excellent dancers, putting me to shame.

We returned to the hospital by carriage. I walked Ruth toward her quarters, taking a long route. The full moon made her beauty even more alluring. This evening had made me forget that I was still in the army, that the war was wearily dragging on south of us, that my companion and I often disagreed in the hospital tents. We stopped to sit awhile on a fallen tree trunk, and I spread out my coat to make a seat for her. Had the wine punch mellowed her? Ruth seemed more friendly than I had ever thought her capable with me.

I moved closer to her and she didn't rebuke me, resting her warm hand on my arm. This caught me by surprise, and I had to take a deep breath. My heart rate increased. That smooth, white hand felt pleasurable on my arm, and I experienced the rapture of love I had not felt since I was with Mary. I kissed her on the cheek, and she turned her head to me and smiled. I kissed her lips, and we looked happily at each other for a minute. I put my arms around her waist and gave her another kiss. Unfortunately, it was late, and she reminded me that she needed to get back to her quarters. Still, it had been an evening of deep feeling. I felt triumphant, bold, nobody that I was. Where now was my rival?

It was early October when the medical inspector from Washington arrived for another inspection of the hospital. He was impressed with the whole hospital, especially my ward. Proudly the stewards, ward masters, nurses, orderlies and I displayed each tent. The tents were all clean, and the patients looked clean and happy, except for the very sick ones. I could not take any of the credit, as Will and Nurse Davenport were the driving forces behind the nursing care. My ward staff was very proud of the kind compliments from the inspector. I had not seen Ruth all day, but she often helped out in other wards when needed. She would have been pleased to hear the inspector's kind remarks. Where could she be?

As I walked the inspector out of our area, we exchanged remarks. "I expect you may have made the acquaintance of Surgeon St. James of the Fifth Corps who had been in Gettysburg during the fighting," he commented. I replied, "Indeed I have, as we both served in the Thirty-Second Massachusetts at that time." "Well," he went on, " Major St. James has met with misfortune, and he was killed in Virginia." I had not expected this news, and I was stunned. "It seems that the Major was racing his horse in a bet with a cavalry private when he fell from his horse and sustained a mortal head injury." I stood speechless as the inspector excused himself and left with the hospital director.

As far as I knew, Ruth had not been notified yet by her relatives or the Sanitary Commission. I was shocked by the news of St. James' death, although, as has been obvious in this narrative, I didn't care for the man. He had, of course, taught me good surgical technique. Guilt pangs were now tugging at my heart. How could I hold a grudge against a dead man and kiss by moonlight the woman he cared for? St. James was a conceited but gifted surgeon. For that matter, he probably had the right to be conceited. He was good enough.

This afternoon I would go by the Sanitary Commission office to see if Ruth had been notified of the untimely death of her doctor friend from Boston. I would try to comfort her in her time of grief.

I never found Miss Davenport that day of the October inspection. She had left Gettysburg earlier in the morning on a train bound for Boston. She didn't even say goodbye or leave a note for me. I mailed a letter to her Cambridge address, but received no reply. She had heard, before I could get to her. And the moment after the ball? Only an idle flirtation and a passing fancy. Her future plans must have died along with St. James.

Chapter IX.

Dedication of Soldiers' National Cemetery
November 19, 1863

October passed quickly and quietly. At the time of the October inspection, the hospital was down to one thousand patients, the number of patients steadily decreasing as they were evacuated to the fixed general hospitals. Our work was concentrated on convalescent care, and as the number of patients decreased, the remaining surgeons were transferred to other assignments.

I must concede that I was jealous of those promoted and reassigned as regimental surgeons. The others were assigned as assistant surgeons in the various general hospitals in Washington, Baltimore, and Philadelphia. I was told I had no reassignment yet and would probably remain at Camp Letterman until it closed in November. Then what would be my fate? I had just about surrendered any chance for an appointment as a regimental surgeon, and thoughts of my own unworthiness invaded my quiet moments.

November came along with the news that the hospital would close on the 20th. There was still no information on promotion or reassignment for me. Only a handful of patients and surgeons remained, all to be transferred to other hospitals. Doctor Maxwell was being reassigned to a general hospital in Washington.

These were uneasy times for me personally, full of self-doubt. I had expected at least to be reassigned to a general hospital. Was I not a decent, even good surgeon? Had I not mastered techniques and saved lives? My patients all liked me. I spoke to Maxwell, who in his usual good-natured way patted me on the back and said not to worry, because I would probably get the best assignment of all.

On the morning of the 19th I was rather dejectedly packing my gear in a shipping trunk. I looked through the great surgery manual by Bernard and Huette which Doctor St. James had loaned me on July 2nd in the Weikert farmhouse, at the time when we were setting up the division field hospital. The book had remained in my possession when he left so suddenly with the regiment. I must have referred to it a hundred times at the Corps Hospital. I placed it in the trunk in memory of my best teacher and harshest critic.

Camp Letterman would be gone by tomorrow afternoon. I re-read my last letter from Mary, full of her wedding plans for December. Why was I keeping this letter and all of the rest? Still, I should probably have no other recourse than to return home, since the army seemed to have forgotten me. I had worked so hard and endured so much, and still I was a failure.

Assistant Surgeon Maxwell and the few remaining surgeons came by my tent in a lively mood and wanted me to go into town with them to Cemetery Hill to attend the dedication of the new Soldiers' National Cemetery there. The President of the United States would be there. I demurred, but they convinced me that I needed the diversion, so they took me along.

We arrived on Cemetery Hill just as Edward Everett was introduced as the main speaker. There was a surprisingly large crowd gathered there that day. Children were running around chasing each other and laughing. One playful little boy ran into me and fell to the ground. He stopped laughing and stared up from the ground at me for a brief moment. I helped him up, and he ran off looking at me all the while as he retreated.

In a few minutes while I was listening to the great orator someone tapped me on the hand. It was the little urchin who had run into me, and with him was Grandma Lizzie, her pretty daughter, all dressed up for the occasion, and the smiling Negro gentleman who ran Lizzie's farm for her. We exchanged pleasantries and they thanked me for coming to Gettysburg to offer succor to the wounded Union troops. True gratitude was in their eyes, for what I and all of the surgeons had done. I felt a new, revivified sense of worth. But I should thank them for what they, too, did voluntarily for our wounded soldiers. I had moist eyes as I extended my hand to each of them. The black gentleman's eyes misted as he looked at me and solemnly shook my hand too.

President Lincoln stood up to give his speech and I craned my neck. The two-hour oration by Edward Everett had worn out the audience; I knew it had me. This was the first time I had ever seen a President. He was reputed to be a tall man and so it did appear, though I was far back in the crowd and could not see him well. When he began to speak, his voice carried rather imperfectly to those of us in the back row. Still, I shall here endeavor to recall my thoughts on that significant utterance, both at the time of its being given and as I had time to ponder the message.

"Four score and seven years ago . . .."

I thought four times twenty is eighty plus seven is eighty-seven years ago and eighty-seven from 1863 is 1776.

And a few sentences later, "Now we are engaged in a great civil war, testing whether that nation, or any nation so conceived and so dedicated, can long endure."

Even after the victories of Gettysburg and Vicksburg, could we be sure? Lee and the Rebels did not recognize the word surrender. Even the President must have been dubious at that moment.

"We are met on a great battlefield of that war. We have come to dedicate a portion of that field, as a final resting place for those who here gave their lives that that nation might live."

And if there be two nations instead of one? Was that so bad? Not bad. Unthinkable.

"It is altogether fitting and proper that we should do this."

Do that—dedicate this field as a cemetery for the members of the Thirty-Second Massachusetts—the freckled, homesick boy—Lieutenant Barrows—all the others. Appropriate without doubt.

"But in a larger sense we can not dedicate, we can not consecrate, we can not hallow this ground. The brave men, living and dead, who struggled here, have consecrated it far above our poor power to add or detract."

Yes. A lot of brave, young lives were ruined here. This would be holy ground now, even if no words were ever said about it. I was upset in general anyway, but I hoped no one would noticed the sensitive tears of this army surgeon.

"The world will little note, nor long remember, what we say here, but it can never forget what they did here."

I vowed to remember them—all I knew and the rest—as long as I was alive. But the world was callous and prone to forget. Seasons would pass, grass grow, and leaves fall on the silent graves here.

"It is for us the living, rather, to be dedicated here to the unfinished work which they who fought here have thus far so nobly advanced."

Would we have the will to complete the task? Many were ready to let the South go on easy terms, anything to stop it all. Political forces were pulling, pulling to give the struggle up.

"It is rather for us to be here dedicated to the great task remaining before us—that from these honored dead we take increased devotion to that cause for which they gave the last full measure of devotion—."

Honored dead. Somehow the faces came before my inner eye and I felt their honor brush off on me, like the pollen of a lily. Surely the saving of a nation of such greatness and destiny was worth the war! It is not always true, as the poet says, that it is sweet and glorious to die for one's country. But at Gettysburg it was least and most certainly glorious. And I knew in a flash that I wasn't a nobody. I had been, was part of a larger effort, and that effort had ennobled us all. Adams had said it: war takes the measure of a man. And right he was: war is not about armaments and taking parcels of land. It is about the testing of a righteous cause in the lives of individual men, and in these cases it is through the cause that we find our own manhood. At least it was so for me. I was a surgeon now, and I knew it.

"That we here highly resolve that these dead shall not have died in vain—that this nation, under God, shall have a new birth of freedom—and that government of the people, by the people, for the people, shall not perish from the earth."

Then he sat back down. That was it? So short? There was a little polite applause scattered among the crowd. A woman in a bonnet next to me whispered about the President's poor efforts in dedicating this great national cemetery for our fallen boys. Still, I must admit I thought it had merit. Who could hear these stirring words without profound emotion? I had come to this place and through participation in its significance had found my life. This I now knew. I turned on my heel, leaving the silly woman and her sneering husband, probably a shirker, behind.

Major Hawthorne, the acting commanding medical officer of Camp Letterman, overtook me on horseback. He called out my name and conveyed a letter to me from the Medical Department. "You'll need to pick up your gear this evening and report to your new regiment." I was puzzled as he rode away, He turned and shouted, "Congratulations Major."

I quickly tore open the letter. The Medical Department was informing me that Governor Oliver P. Morton of Indiana had an appointment for me to the rank of Major as Surgeon of a new Indiana volunteer infantry regiment being raised in Indianapolis. Should I accept, I was to resign immediately as a U. S. Volunteer Assistant Surgeon and return to Indiana in all haste. If not, I would be reassigned to a general hospital. I was instructed to telegraph my reply within twenty-four hours and proceed at once to my new regiment. This was a moment of fulfillment I had long awaited, and I proceeded at once to the camp to pick up my things and get to the railroad depot for my trip back home.

By the time I arrived at Camp Letterman it had all but vanished from the face of the earth. All of the hospital tents were gone. The possessions of the remaining staff were already loaded in wagons. Ah, well, *sic transit gloria mundi.* I was informed by the man guarding the wagons that there was a train out early in the morning, and my gear would be delivered to the depot tonight. My work was finished here. I was free to go.

I said farewell to the remaining medical staff and spoke briefly with Major Hawthorne. "Goodbye, Doctor Baldwin. Congratulations on your appointment as a regimental surgeon, and good luck," he said. I told him, "I don't understand why Governor Morton would suddenly give me an appointment as regimental surgeon. There must be cousins or Centerville neighbors he could have appointed."

Then came Hawthorne's startling revelation to me. "Surgeon Theodore St. James wrote a letter of recommendation to Governor Morton citing your skill and dedication at Gettysburg and urging the governor to give you an appointment as regimental surgeon. He said you had more than proven yourself under fire as a competent surgeon."

Major Hawthorne left me to my silence. I walked into the woods a bit. There was something redeeming in what I had just been told about St. James. I felt a little guilty; he was gone now, and I had never even had the chance to thank him. If I knew him, though, he'd be sardonically satisfied with my unease over his unexpected beneficence.

Then I thought of Ruth and wondered if she would ever find happiness.

I started walking down familiar York Pike to Gettysburg for the last time. I felt lonely; everyone in the hospital had already scattered or were in the process of leaving town. As I reached the town square, my eyes looked north towards the railroad depot, but then my legs turned south on Baltimore Street. The townsfolk were preoccupied and busy with their daily routine. They seemed not to notice a lone Union surgeon walking through their quiet and peaceful little town.

There, there they were, the houses, stores, and churches that had seen such traumatic agony. Many of the buildings had bullet holes and pock marks on the bricks as reminders of those three terrible days in July. Here Ewell had stood, surrounded by angry-faced generals who had shouted at him to invest the hill. There, over there, the Northern boys had run, chased by Southerners, hiding between buildings. And there, back at the railroad depot, the hospital where the surgeon of the Iron Brigade and others had tried to get through the night with supplies allowed through the lines. Gone, all gone now.

I walked on south of town down Emmitsburg Road, and turned left on the Wheatfield Road at the peach orchard. I took a winding farm trail south of the road to the stony hill. Where was I being drawn? My eyes sought familiar ground, but it all appeared different now. The grass was brown. It had been tall and green when I was here before. The trees were without their leaves, and had been full of summer green when I first saw this place. The Thirty-Second Massachusetts had been around here somewhere. I became filled with disappointment; I couldn't find our line of battle. The boulders had to be around here somewhere. I could see the wheatfield nearby.

Yes, here were the boulders. The dressing station must have been here at this almost hidden site. And the regiment had lined up down there and was struck by the Confederates, there, down there. Our dressing station was an obscure little spot, and the world might not ever remember or care what happened to us here. We had been a family, the Thirty-Second Massachusetts. Some of them now lay forever in the new national cemetery. "The world will little note, nor long remember—"

Bright young rural sons of Concord, tradesmen of Tremont Street in Boston, and fishers from the wind-blown towns facing the sea stretches around Plum Island——a unit, soon to be scattered to the wind like the chaff of the wheat that was never harvested here.

On an impulse, I took out my pocket knife and proceeded to scratch on a stony surface, "DRESSING STATION—32ND MASS." The words were hardly readable, and would not last long. Surgeon Adams and Assistant Surgeon St. James—Colonel Prescott, Captain Garceau, Lieutenant Barrows, Chaplain O'Mara, Steward Franz, Corporal Phillips, and the homesick private had all made an indelible mark here. The rains of coming seasons and the indifference of coming generations could not erase what they had done, as the President had said. Yes, as he said about us all.

Solemn sadness swept over me and made me glad to be leaving this killing ground at last. Perhaps I would come back here from time to time to remember and visit the men I knew here, in this quiet country place.

So now there will be a memorial to those hours of triumph and hell. I thank you on behalf of the comrades I came to know for your desire for permanent commemoration and pray all good success for your laudable effort.

Epilogue

The monument to the Thirty-Second Massachusetts Infantry is located on the stony hill near the wheatfield. It is in the shape of a shelter tent. The Thirty-Second went into line of battle at this location on July 2, 1863.

HERE THE
32ᴰ·MASSACHUSETTS INFY.
2ᴺᴰ BRIG. 1ˢᵀ DIV. 5ᵀᴴA.C.
WITHSTOOD AN ATTACK OF THE ENEMY
ABOUT 5 0'CLOCK P.M. JULY 2, 1863.

WITHDRAWN FROM HERE IT FOUGHT AGAIN IN THE
WHEATFIELD.
IT LOST IN BOTH ACTIONS IN KILLED AND WOUNDED
78 OUT OF 227 OFFICERS AND MEN.

About one-hundred yards to the rear, eastward, there is a bronze plaque placed on a large boulder in a group of boulders which provided shelter for the dressing station.

BEHIND THIS GROUP OF ROCKS,
ON THE AFTERNOON OF JULY 2ND, 1863,
SURGEON Z. BOYLSTON ADAMS
PLACED THE FIELD HOSPITAL OF THE
32ND-MASSACHUSETTS INFANTRY,
2ND BRIGADE, 1ST DIV., 5TH ARMY CORPS.
ESTABLISHED SO NEAR THE LINE
OF BATTLE, MANY OF OUR WOUNDED
ESCAPED CAPTURE OR DEATH BY ITS
TIMELY AID.

PLACED BY THE
VETERAN ASSOCIATION OF THE REGIMENT.

The monument of the Thirty-Second Massachusetts Infantry can be located on Sickles Avenue at the loop on the stony hill near the wheatfield. It is a unique monument in the shape of a shelter tent. The Thirty-Second went into line of battle at this location on July 2, 1863, at about 5 pm.

The bronze plaque to the dressing station of Surgeon Z. Boylston Adams can be located in the group of large boulders just behind the monument of the Fifth Michigan Infantry on Sickles Avenue about 120 paces east from the monument of the Thirty-Second Massachusetts Infantry.

POSTSCRIPT

On my first few visits to Gettysburg, I saw a great battlefield with monuments to the gallant armies, generals, and soldiers who fought there for the first three days of July in 1863. On a later visit while on a downtown walking tour, I saw churches and other buildings which had been used as hospitals to treat the thousands of wounded soldiers from both sides. I also bought a book by Gregory A. Coco, *A Vast Sea of Misery*, (Thomas Publications, 1988.) This book became a complete guide to tour the battlefield for sites of medical interest.

After the battle, the armies went south, but about 21,000 wounded soldiers were left behind in Gettysburg. The last wounded soldier was not evacuated from the town until late November. As an orthopaedic surgeon who had also served in the U. S. Army Medical Corps in a general hospital in Tokyo from 1968-1971, I became very interested in the medical aspects of Gettysburg. I then saw Gettysburg from a medical viewpoint as well as a military one. The meaning of Gettysburg to me has never been quite the same after that.

When I see battle lines I wonder where the dressing stations might have been set up by the assistant surgeons. I see churches, houses, and barns as field hospitals. I wonder what it must have been like to have been a wounded soldier and to have undergone an amputation with only light chloroform anesthesia. I wonder what it must have been like to have been an operating surgeon doing amputations all night long under candle light among the moans of the mortally wounded and all of the blood and filth. I suppose we will never know.

The following references were especially helpful to me: Adams, G.W., *Doctors in Blue*, Morningside House Inc., 1985; Billings, J.D., *Hardtack and Coffee*, George M. Smith & Co., 1887 (reprinted Time-Life

Scribner's Sons, 1984; Dammann, G., *A Pictorial Encyclopedia of Civil War Medical Instruments and Equipment.* Vol. I & II, Pictorial Histories Publishing Co., 1990; Garrison, F.H., *John Shaw Billings - A Memoir.* The Knickerbocker Press, 1915; *The Medical and Surgical History of the Civil War.* Broadfoot Publishing Co., 1991; Parker, F.J., *The Story of the Thirty-Second Regiment Massachusetts Infantry.* C.W. Calkins & Co., 1880; Peabody, C.N., *ZAB: (Brevet Major Zabdiel Boylston Adams, 1829-1902, Physician of Boston and Framingham).* The Francis A. Countway Library of Medicine, 1984; Pfanz, H.W., *Gettysburg - The Second Day.* The University of North Carolina Press, 1987; Smith, S., *Hand-Book of Surgical Operations.* Bailliere Brothers, 1862 (reprinted Norman Publishing, 1990); and Woodward, J.J., *The Hospital Steward's Manual.* Lippincott, 1862 (reprinted Norman Publishing, 1991).

My publisher, Nancy N. Baxter, has done a superb job in guiding and helping me to transform my ideas into this book. Her expertise is much appreciated.

I want to give a special thanks to Nancy L. Eckerman, Special Collections Librarian, Ruth Lilly Medical Library, Indiana University School of Medicine, for her valuable assistance and advice. Also, I have learned a lot by watching reenactors bring the look and feel of the Civil War back to life for the American public.

My special thanks go to Dr. Gary W. Gallagher for his Penn State Mont Alto Civil War Conferences on Gettysburg and for reading my manuscript. His positive response encouraged me in the final phases of this work.

Finally, I want to thank my wife, Mary, and my children, Kim, Shannon, and Kevin, for encouraging my interest in the Civil War and buying me more books than I can read.

Clyde B. Kernek, M.D.
July 4, 1993

A Memorial Account

Clyde B. Kernek is an Associate Professor of Orthopaedic Surgery at Indiana University School of Medicine in Indianapolis. He served in the U. S. Army Medical Corps in Tokyo, Japan, treating soldiers with war wounds from 1968 to 1971. His interest in the Civil War includes the medical and surgical aspects of this period in American history.

Clyde lives in Carmel, Indiana, with his wife, Mary. They have three grown children.